Could this be Love?
I Wondered

Marilyn Taylor

The O'Brien Press
DUBLIN

First published 1994 by The O'Brien Press Ltd.,
20 Victoria Road, Rathgar, Dublin 6, Ireland.

British Library Cataloguing-in-publication Data
A catalogue reference for this title is available from the British Library

ISBN 0-86278-377-1

10 9 8 7 6 5 4 3 2

Cover illustration: Donald Teskey
Cover design: The O'Brien Press
Cover separations: Lithoset Ltd., Dublin
Printing: Cox & Wyman Ltd., Reading

CONTENTS

For Mervyn, Adam, Maryanne, Gideon and Debbie,
and for Kieran, Anne and Diana,
with appreciation for all their help,
encouragement and support

The Look

He was at the bus stop again today.

It was another grey, wet Monday morning. I peered out through the dirty steamed-up window of the bus and immediately our eyes met and held in a long Look. His straight fair hair was plastered down from the rain and he was wearing the same denim jacket with faded jeans and grubby trainers.

My friend Deirdre noticed my sudden silence. 'The mystery man again?' she asked, her eyes following mine.

Wet people piled into the bus until it was full. It jerked and started off, leaving a crowd behind at the stop, including him. I felt stirred up and peculiar, as I always did after The Look. I wondered if we were ever going to get any further.

Deirdre was obviously thinking along similar lines. 'He must live in Ballytymon,' she said. 'Surely you can track him down?'

I had already worked this out for myself. I'd seen him

a few times getting off the Ballytymon bus or waiting at our stop for the bus into town. The problem was that thousands of people lived in Ballytymon. I pointed this out to Deirdre. Ever-helpful, she tried again.

'You could get out at his bus stop some morning – '

'And then what?' I asked cuttingly. 'Go up to him and say it's time we got beyond The Look? Anyway I'd be late for school and I've already had two late slips this term. My dad'll give out.' This was a bit unfair to Dad who's usually too rushed to give out to me unless prompted by Mum.

'You've got to allow the relationship to develop naturally,' said Deirdre, who spent a lot of her time reading the 'Dear Anne' column in *Teen Dreams*.

'What relationship? Maybe it's not really a Look, he might just be short-sighted. Or perhaps he's got something wrong with his eyes that stops him blinking. He never seems to smile.'

Actually, his seriousness was part of his attraction. He appeared so different from other boys who were usually showing off, teasing or messing around.

Later, in French class, I chewed my pen and drew a picture of him in the back of *Français Aujourd'hui*, which already contained a portrait gallery of almost everyone I knew. I'd even done my younger brother. I must have been bored to desperation that day.

The bell rang and I went to my locker to get my lunch and meet Deirdre. She came rushing up the stairs, her face flushed, long dark hair flying.

It's a pain sometimes, your best friend being so pretty. She always looks great, even dressed from head to foot in the peculiar shade of turquoise which is the colour of our school uniform.

I felt ashamed of the flash of envy when she hurried over and gasped breathlessly, 'There's a disco next Saturday in a school in Ballytymon, your man might be there. Therese says we can go with her, she lives quite near. We can stay in her house.'

'In Ballytymon? The corporation estates? You must be joking, my parents would never let me,' I said. Why do I always come out with these negative replies? Deirdre says I'm a pessimist. But it often seems safer to look on the black side, then you can't be too disappointed.

Deirdre looked impatient. 'It's not that far from Rathnure,' she said. 'And it's in a school, so you can tell them it's supervised.'

'I'll try,' I answered. Think positively, I added silently to myself.

* * *

When I got home the house was quiet. Mum's white Toyota Starlet, newly washed, was sitting in the driveway.

The garden was neat, the grass freshly cut, daffodils and tulips flowering in little clumps between the rose bushes. It was obvious the gardener had been. The leafy Dublin suburb of Rathnure where we lived was noted for its gardens and Mum and Mr Cottrell, the gardener, put in hours of work, without much help from the rest of us.

I went through the side door and let myself into the kitchen. There was a plate on the table with chocolate cake covered with clingfilm, and a note from Mum saying she had gone to do Meals on Wheels.

I took a can of Coke from the fridge and went up to my room. When I'd put on U2's 'Zooropa' I sat at my desk munching absently, thinking about The Look at the bus stop, until the front door banged and Mum called up, 'Turn down that noise, Jackie, the house is shaking!' She says that every day.

I lowered the volume and went downstairs. My mother looked neat and smart as always, her hair swept back, highlights gleaming. I thought of my thick wiry mop of hair which always looks the same, no matter how carefully I blow-dry it.

'How was school?' Mum asked brightly. She asks that every day, too.

'All right,' I replied. 'The usual.'

I took a deep breath, but before I could say anything there was a massive crash as the back door burst open and my brother Philip appeared. He flung his overflowing schoolbag on to the floor. Mum sighed.

'How was school?' she asked him, a bit less brightly.

He grunted something non-committal and stretched out a dirty hand to grab a piece of cake from the table. With his mouth full he muttered something that sounded like 'football match', and banged out.

Mum and I exchanged glances.

I took another deep breath. 'Mum, Deirdre's asked me to go to a disco on Saturday. Loads of people from school are going.'

'Where is it?' she asked.

'In a school in Ballytymon.'

'Ballytymon?' she repeated, as if I'd said Outer Space. There was a pause. 'How on earth would you get there?'

'It's not that far.' I echoed Deirdre. 'We can stay the night with Therese from our class.'

Mum looked anxious. 'It's in a school. And it's supervised,' I said, using the magic words.

'And you say Deirdre and some others from school are going?'

'Yes,' I said, hoping they were. My parents approved of Deirdre. Her father was a dentist and her mother was active in Fine Gael.

There was another pause. Then Mum said, 'I'll have to speak to your father.'

I knew the battle was won. 'Your hair looks nice,' I said.

The Disco

Well, the disco was great, but he wasn't there.

My dad drove Deirdre, me and Ruth. Ruth is one of our gang at school. She's really cool except when she's giving us advice about vitamins and additives and what foods we ought to eat. Mind you, this doesn't stop her going on about her own health and how she's feeling. This time she told us gloomily about the cough which she said had kept her up all night.

We often slagged her about all the complaints, but Deirdre said that according to the health column in *Teen Dreams* Ruth might be a hypochondriac. Apparently that means a lot of your ailments are imaginary.

'It's to get attention,' Deirdre had said knowingly. It reminded me of my gran talking about my brother Philip when he'd done something infuriating.

I stared out of the car window at the thick fog, which Dad gave out about all the way up the Ballytymon road.

'They're supposed to have got rid of this damned smog.

I mean, we're paying the highest taxes in Europe,' he announced to a silent car.

Ruth coughed away in the back. I often wonder who 'they' are – my dad always seems angry with them.

We found the school after asking several people for directions. Dad hates doing that, he usually drives off while they're still talking, and they're left open-mouthed. It's really embarrassing.

He dropped us off, forgetting to get the address of Therese's house where we were staying the night. Mum wouldn't be pleased about that. She's always worrying about Philip and me, especially after the recent 'Gay Byrne Show', when there'd been loads of letters from listeners blaming parents for young people getting into trouble.

Clustering together nervously outside the swing doors of the school we watched Dad drive off. We were all dressed to kill, Ruth in wild flowery leggings and a long baggy sweater which she'd borrowed from her sister, and Deirdre in a white body and a tiny white mini-skirt which she said had her legs frozen. I was all in black, and although I'd used about a pint of mousse my hair looked as though I'd been electrocuted. At least, that was what my darling brother had said before we'd left.

Loud rock music was blaring through the closed doors. We waited outside shivering till Therese's arrival perked us up.

Therese is always trying to persuade us to go to assertiveness classes with her. We may need to, but she's definitely assertive enough already. She rounded us up and swept us inside.

*   *   *

My heart always sinks when I go into a crowded room, even if I know everyone. Here I couldn't see even one familiar face. There seemed to be loads of people, mostly girls about our age, dressed much like us.

A girl left one of the noisy groups and came over. She had beautiful long fair hair which swung as she walked. 'Hi,' she shouted to Therese over the music. She looked at us curiously. 'Are these the kids from your school?'

'Yeah – Jackie, Deirdre and Ruth. This is Bernie, she lives on my road. Where're the lads?'

'Still hanging round the chipper,' answered Bernie apologetically. We smiled understandingly. They do that at our school discos too.

We all went down to a bar at the far end of the room. I was surprised to find there were only Cokes, Pepsis and orange. After Mum's dire warnings I'd imagined drink flowing, drugs being handed out. This was disappointingly like the discos in our school.

We sipped the drinks. Ruth coughed and said she could feel a headache coming on. Deirdre and I ignored her and looked around. A group of grown-ups were surveying the scene.

'Who are they?' I asked Bernie.

'They're our teachers – the one in jeans is my class

teacher, Miss O'Reilly. We call her Mags.'

As we watched, Miss O'Reilly was dragged on to the floor to dance by a boy with a shaved head and one earring. She waved airily at Bernie as they bopped past.

Deirdre and I looked at each other amazed. Maybe it wasn't quite like our school after all. I couldn't imagine Sister Imelda doing that, or even Miss Kinsella.

A good-looking guy in a leather jacket approached. He said to Bernie, 'Lads still at the chipper, I suppose?' He smiled at us. 'You must be from Therese's school. You're very welcome to Ballytymon. Sorry about the lads. I think I'd better go and round them up.'

'He's gorgeous,' said Deirdre, watching admiringly as he strode off. 'Is he a teacher too?'

'Yeah. All the girls fancy him, but he's married,' replied Bernie. 'They've a really cute baby – everyone's desperate to babysit because he drives you home.'

Miss O'Reilly danced past again, this time with a short boy wearing glasses, whose pink face was shining with sweat. 'Hi, Bernie, Therese,' she shouted, 'lads still at the chipper?'

* * *

The lads finally arrived in a bunch. The leather-jacketed teacher looked a bit like a sheep-dog nudging a crowd of unwilling sheep. I scanned their faces, noticing Deirdre doing the same, but there was no sign of the one we were looking for.

Even so they turned out to be great crack. Deirdre got off with a real hunk called Andy, who asked her to meet him the next night. She's already got a boyfriend from the boys' school beside ours and I knew she was supposed to be meeting him. I couldn't believe it when I heard her say yes.

'*Deirdre*,' I hissed when Andy went to get a drink, 'what about Mark?'

She raised her eyebrows and opened her eyes wide. 'Mark who?' she asked sweetly.

* * *

Walking home together was fun. Everyone seemed to live near each other.

I found myself beside Bernie, the one with the swinging fair hair. She was really friendly, and told me she had an older brother and three little sisters. She'd practically brought up the sisters because her mother had trouble with her nerves and often had to go to St Loman's for treatment.

'What about your dad?' I asked.

'He's gone to England. We hardly ever hear from him,' she answered.

I couldn't help feeling a bit shocked at this. I wasn't sure what to say. But Bernie didn't seem to notice. She said matter-of-factly that she thought her dad had a woman in England and he didn't care about them any more.

'Don't you mind?' As soon as I said it I thought how brainless it sounded.

But Bernie just shrugged. 'We do the best we can. My

ma feels it worst. You don't get much from the Social Welfare. My brother had to leave school. He got a job in a burger place in Castlemines. That's been a help.'

I thought this over. I couldn't imagine my dad going to England and forgetting about us. On the other hand he was always so busy and harassed-looking, and he often said irritably, 'D'you think I'm made of money?' Perhaps money might be a problem for us too, but no-one ever admitted it.

I could hear Ruth chatting away behind me. She hadn't coughed for ages and she seemed to have forgotten about the headache.

When we got to Therese's house Bernie came in with us for a while. It was after one o'clock and I was ready to creep in quietly like I did at home, so as not to disturb anyone. But the house was brightly lit and full of people. Therese's mum and dad were in the kitchen chatting cheerfully with some neighbours, and her brothers were in the living-room watching a video with a crowd of friends. We were all welcomed and given tea and sand-wiches which we wolfed down hungrily.

After Bernie left we squashed into Therese's small bedroom upstairs and talked for ages. Ruth and Therese said the hunky teacher in the leather jacket had suggested that we should start visits between our school discos to get to know each other better. We all thought it sounded like a good idea, though I wasn't sure what Miss Kinsella would think.

Deirdre told us she'd fallen in love with Andy the hunk and she now realised that Mark was immature and a bit boring too.

'A sense of humour is vital in a partner,' she said firmly. Sounded like the 'Dear Anne' column again!

Then I told them that Bernie said she'd meet us after school on Thursday and bring us to Burgerama where her brother worked. We might get free burgers. That received general approval, except from Ruth who went on about burgers being unhealthy because of all the fat and artificial colours and flavourings.

Eventually, to the sound of talk and laughter from downstairs, we drifted off to sleep.

I dreamed about the mystery man at the bus stop. Funny, I thought I'd started to forget about him.

The Encounter

It was Monday morning again. I was sitting beside Ruth and drawing another portrait in my French book, this time of Bernie. It was quite difficult to catch the swing of her hair and her serene expression. Ruth looked over at it with a smile of recognition and then clutched her jaw. She had a toothache today.

The French teacher bore down on us and I turned hastily to reflexive verbs.

But when I'd finished the French exercise my thoughts kept returning to the disco in Ballytymon, and then to the events of the following day.

*   *   *

It had started like the usual boring Sunday at home, with a loud clattering of plates from the kitchen.

Mum is never in good form on Sundays because my two grandmothers usually come for lunch. They aren't a bit alike, but Philip or I usually manage to annoy one or other of them. Philip's worse than me though.

I set the table and answered Mum's snapped questions about the disco in monosyllables. I know how irritating that is when Philip does it, but I just couldn't describe all the details.

The whole evening had been ordinary in a way, but so many things had left an impression, the laid-back teachers, the unexpected friendliness, the welcome at Therese's house, Bernie's honesty and the way she accepted her family problems so calmly.

The doorbell rang and I went to answer it.

Gran, Dad's mother, gave me a hug and exclaimed how well I looked. She believes in giving young people a positive image of themselves. It's great for the ego, even when it isn't quite accurate.

Nana arrived shortly afterwards and gave us each a peck on the cheek. 'Jackie's getting quite grown up,' she remarked to my mother as they all sipped glasses of sherry. 'Shouldn't you do something about her hair? It needs a proper cut and shape. I could bring her to Marcel.'

'I think her hair looks nice,' said Gran. 'It's the way they wear it these days. Aggro or something isn't it, dear?'

'You mean Afro, Gran, and anyway, it's not,' I muttered.

'Perhaps if she got it thinned and layered,' my mother mused. They all looked critically at my hair.

I escaped into the kitchen and found my brother wolfing down a large piece of chicken off one of the plates set out on the table. He jumped guiltily. 'Greedy pig,' I snapped.

'You really must do something about your hair,' he shrilled in Nana's voice. 'Why not try the latest baldy look? Marcel will do it for you.'

My mother came in slightly flushed from the sherry. She bustled around the kitchen. 'You children go in and talk to your grans,' she said. 'You don't see them that often.' Philip made a face behind Mum's back.

'I'm fed up with everyone going on about my hair,' I grumbled. 'Why don't they talk about Philip's hair, or his filthy nails?' He clenched his fists.

Mum put on her apron and started dishing out the soup.

Deirdre phoned when we'd just finished lunch. She was having cold feet about meeting Andy the hunk that evening and wanted Ruth and me to go along.

'Okay,' I said, 'if you don't mind arriving with two minders.'

'And what am I going to say to Mark?' she wailed.

'Mark who?' I said innocently.

* * *

In fact Sunday night worked out fine. Andy had a couple of the lads with him for moral support as well. We all went to the local cinema in Rathnure and saw a disgusting horror film.

Andy was a bit full of himself at first, but he simmered down after some chilling looks from us. He's really good-looking but the trouble is he knows it. Deirdre seems to be mad about him.

He certainly can be really funny and he entertained us with stories about Dunnes Stores where he works at weekends.

He said it was dead embarrassing having to wear a label saying 'Andy'. Then he told us that last night he and the lads had been intercepted by the teacher with the leather jacket just as they were about to sneak round to the off-licence to try and get a six pack to smuggle into the disco. Apparently every time they try it they're frustrated by the shopowner or by a vigilant teacher.

'They should be in the Special Branch,' he complained.

Afterwards I couldn't help thinking it was ironic that we'd gone to the disco to look for my mystery man, and Deirdre had ended up with a new boyfriend. It's the story of my life.

*   *   *

Thursday, the day Bernie was coming from Ballytymon to meet us, was a lovely spring day. We met at the shopping centre after school, laden down with bags and tennis rackets.

Bernie looked brilliant in jeans and a long cotton sweater, her hair shining. I felt hideous in my uniform. We all strolled slowly towards Castlemines, with Ruth, who said she'd hurt her ankle in PE, limping along behind. I could hear Therese reminding her unkindly that at least the sore ankle seemed to have cured the toothache.

You couldn't miss Burgerama with its huge flashing

neon sign. We crowded in and Bernie looked around for her brother. She headed over to the brightly-lit counter and spoke to someone behind it. Then she beckoned us over.

I looked beyond her to the tall fair-haired boy wearing a striped apron. I felt a sudden jolt and my stomach churned as our eyes met.

It was him! Bernie's brother was my mystery man.

* * *

Bernie didn't notice my confusion but Deirdre gave me an enormous nudge with her elbow which nearly knocked me over, weak at the knees as I was.

'This is my brother Kev,' said Bernie.

He said 'Howya' to us all, but his eyes remained on me.

The next hour passed like a dream. Bernie ordered burgers, French fries and Cokes and we took them over to a table. After a bit Kev came over and I was able to look at him properly, though I still felt a bit peculiar. He wasn't as good-looking as Andy but he had lovely grey eyes and the serious expression, and the same straight fair hair as Bernie.

I had pictured myself meeting him in all kinds of situations, but I certainly hadn't bargained on being decked out in my awful turquoise uniform.

Just as I began to get a panicky feeling that the whole thing was going to peter out in a dreadful anticlimax, he came up behind my chair, bent down and whispered, 'I've seen you in Rathnure.'

I turned round. His face was on a level with mine. The only reply I could think of was 'Yeah' which seemed pretty feeble. I tried furiously to think of what to say next, but my mind was blank.

Then he said, 'D'ya want to get together some time?'

I managed to mumble, 'That'd be cool.' I really meant it'd be brilliant, but that might sound too eager. Still, at least I'd finally said something, though it was hardly scintillating. I hurried on, 'Why don't you phone me? I'll give Bernie the number.'

There was a sudden silence, and I realised the whole table was listening. He muttered, 'See ya,' and rushed off.

After a moment they all started talking again, a bit too loudly. I sat on in a kind of rosy glow, hearing them talking but not what they were saying.

Could this be love? I wondered.

The Call

The phone rang.

I jumped up from my desk which was littered with school books.

I was supposed to be doing my homework. I'd written two paragraphs of an English essay on the Romantic poets. The third paragraph consisted of drawings of Zig and Zag, and the names 'Kev' and 'Kev and Jackie' in several different kinds of handwriting.

I opened my bedroom door slightly and heard Mum chatting to her sister, my Auntie Gemma, in Galway. Auntie Gemma has recently had a hysterectomy. Although Mum seems to think I shouldn't even know what a hysterectomy is, in fact I've learnt more about female reproductive organs from overhearing their phone conversations than from years of biology lessons.

* * *

It was now Saturday evening and I hadn't heard from Kev. I knew that Therese would advise me to assert myself and phone him. But his sister Bernie had told me that they had no phone at home. And I didn't think I could work up the confidence to ring him at Burgerama.

I'd had hundreds of imaginary conversations with him. But I knew if the call came I'd have trouble finding anything to say.

The phone rang again and my heart jumped as Mum called me. But it was Deirdre.

'Oh, it's you,' I said, not even trying to hide my disappointment.

'Don't be so enthusiastic,' she said. 'I suppose you thought it was him. So he hasn't phoned?'

I thought of asking who she meant, but I knew it was useless. Practically the whole of my class at school was following developments with breathless interest. Discretion was not Deirdre's strong point.

'No,' I answered.

Deirdre ignored my tone. 'I hear that Bernie told Therese that her brother might be seeing you tonight.'

My heart jumped again. It was ridiculous to be so up and down over someone I hardly knew. I wish I was a calm person who takes everything in their stride, like Bernie.

'It's the first I've heard,' I said. Then I remembered about Andy. If this is love, it makes you very self-centred.

'Heard anything from Andy?' I asked.

'No.' Deirdre sounded a bit down.

'Fellas are a pain,' I said comfortingly. 'Let's have an all girls' evening.'

'Right,' she replied, cheering up. 'Meet you at Ruth's at half eight. I can't wait to escape. My mum's having a Fine Gael coffee morning tomorrow and the place is full of sponge cakes.'

I was about to hang up when she added, 'By the way, Ruth's ankle and tooth are better but she thinks she's got a grumbling appendix.'

As I put the phone down it rang immediately. I picked it up. There was a silence and I held my breath.

A muffled voice said, 'Er – Jackie there?' I knew instantly it was him.

'Yes, it's me.' My voice sounded shrill. I tried to lower it a few tones.

'It's Kev,' he said unnecessarily.

'I know.' There was a silence.

'Howya,' he said. Another silence. What could I say?

'How's things?' He must be amazed at my brilliant wit.

'Can't talk – I'm in work. Can you meet me at Pizza Paradise in Rathnure when I get off 'round nine?'

My mind raced. I couldn't leave Deirdre and the others high and dry. But if I said no he might be discouraged and never ask again. But he needn't have left it so late to phone.

'I'm meeting Deirdre and Ruth. Is it okay if they come?' Maybe they'd go off after a while.

'Sure,' he said. 'The lads'll be down too.'

The lads, I thought. Our relationship was not going to have much of a chance to develop, as Deirdre would put it, if my crowd and the lads were going to be around all the time. Still, at least I'd be seeing him. It was a start. Don't look on the black side, I told myself.

'Will Andy be there?' I asked Kev.

'Yeah,' he paused for a second. 'You can tell your friend.'

So he knew about Deirdre and Andy. I wondered if he'd discussed me with the lads, and if so, what they'd said. At least I had a bit of good news to give Deirdre, although Andy might have talked to her himself.

I noticed that the kitchen door was open. There was a suspicious silence from inside. I knew Mum would soon be asking some over-casual questions.

'Bye, see ya,' I said hastily, and put the phone down.

Philip barged out of the kitchen. "Who was that?" he asked loudly.

'None of your business,' I muttered.

He raised his voice. 'If it's a guy, what's his name, where's he live, what's his father do, where are you meeting him, what colour is his hair, where –'

'Oh, shut up,' I shouted and rushed upstairs.

If this was love, it was really stressful. Especially with a brother like Philip.

The Date

He was half an hour late at Pizza Paradise.

Deciding what to wear had been difficult. In the end I'd put on my black leggings and a huge purple and black striped sweatshirt borrowed from Deirdre, which Mum thought was two sizes too big for me and Dad said should be given to the St Vincent de Paul.

The place was packed. It was popular with our crowd because as well as takeaway there were tables where you could sit and talk, and a video jukebox.

Andy came sauntering over when we arrived. You could see Deirdre forgiving him instantly for not bothering to ring her, though she'd been complaining about him on the way over.

We got some slices of pizza at the counter and brought them to the table. Deirdre said the fella who was serving looked like Daniel Day Lewis. Andy said Daniel Day Lewis was rubbish. I thought to myself that Andy could really get on your nerves. But Deirdre didn't seem to mind. I hope love doesn't mean you never have a mind of your own any more.

Ruth was deep in conversation with two of the lads. I remembered the one with an earring from the disco. He was describing in detail how he puked after his fourth turn on the Ramba Zamba in Funderland. Ruth was a bit pale.

Then I heard her say, 'I always wanted to go to Funderland.' It didn't seem to me the most suitable place for someone who felt sick even on the bus. I dreaded to think what the Ramba Zamba would do to her.

Everyone except me seemed to be getting on brilliantly. But I was beginning to wonder if Kev was going to show up.

Then Therese, who had just come from her assertiveness class, strode in forcefully and took the only empty seat at the table. She was followed by Bernie, her shining hair tied back with a black gauzy scarf.

As soon as I could catch Bernie's attention I said, 'Hi,' and added, in a whisper, 'Is Kev coming?'

Just then he walked in. Our eyes met, just like they did at the bus stop. My heart lurched in the unsettling way that I was getting used to. Deirdre gave me a nudge without taking her eyes off Andy.

'All right,' I hissed, 'I'm not blind.'

Kev gave us a casual wave and went straight over to the lads. I watched, annoyed. He hadn't even said hi.

Bernie said quietly, 'Don't mind him. He'll be over now in a minute.'

Sure enough after a few moments he appeared behind my chair. 'Comin' out?' he said, unsmiling.

Bernie whispered to me as he moved off, 'You just have to give him time.'

Wondering if she read the 'Dear Anne' column like Deirdre, I smiled back at her and followed Kev outside.

As we left I noticed Deirdre and Ruth exchanging a knowing glance.

*   *   *

Outside, away from the noise and steam of Pizza Paradise, it was cool and quiet. We walked slowly towards Rathnure village.

It was the first time we'd been alone. As usual my mind was a blank. I looked down at my black ankle boots and his dirty trainers.

'Where d'you live?' he asked. I told him. There was a silence.

I asked him if he liked working in Burgerama. It was the sort of stupid question parents usually ask.

He shrugged. 'It's all right.' Another silence.

I searched desperately for something to say. Then I remembered what Bernie had told me after the disco.

I blurted, 'Did you mind having to leave school?'

He stopped dead. 'How d'you know about that?'

My heart sank. Trust me to say the wrong thing. I answered nervously, 'Bernie told me.'

He said nothing.

Then I thought, are we going to go on forever with these deadly silences? I took a deep breath to give myself some courage. 'She also told me about your dad leaving and your mum feeling bad. It must be hard for you and Bernie. I don't have any big problems like that at home.' Thinking about Philip, the exams looming, my hair, the Romantic poets, I added, 'I've got lots of smaller ones though.'

For a moment he said nothing. I wondered if I'd messed up everything. He looked directly at me for the first time that evening.

And then he suddenly smiled. I'd never seen him really smile properly, and I felt a sort of warm glow inside. After that it was as though we'd broken through a barrier. He told me he'd quite liked school, which seemed a bit weird to me. He talked about his mum and how depressed she was since their dad left. The Valium had seemed to help her at first, but as she took more and more pills she was less and less able to cope with the kids and everything else.

'Bernie's brilliant,' he said. 'She helps with the kids and the messages. I do a bit when I can.' I couldn't imagine my brother Philip ever saying anything like that about me.

I told him about Deirdre and the gang and school and the disco in Ballytymon. He didn't say much but he listened. I felt as though I could tell him anything, all the things I was always worrying about. I even told him how Nana went on about my hair.

'Your hair's all right,' he said, looking at it with his serious expression.

We talked about parents. 'They're so protective,' I said, 'Especially my mum. I know they care about me and all that, but sometimes I feel smothered. My brother Philip would have you driven mad. And my dad hardly says anything these days.'

Then I thought, maybe I sounded a bit spoilt. Even if Dad was usually silent and preoccupied, he was there when we needed him, and so were Mum and even the two grans. Kev and Bernie and their mum and the younger kids had to look after themselves.

We walked for a while without saying anything, but it wasn't awkward like before.

'My dad's got some woman in England,' Kev said suddenly, looking straight ahead.

'D'you ever see him?' I asked.

'He sends money sometimes, but I tell Ma to send it back.' His voice hardened. 'He doesn't give a shit about us.'

He walked faster and faster and I had to nearly run to keep up. I said, breathlessly, 'What about your mum?'

'She never stood up to him. She always took him back when he showed up and said he was off the drink.'

His expression was fierce. 'We don't need his bleedin' money,' he said bitterly.

He slowed down, and I thought how different this conversation was from any I had with my other friends. Deirdre and the others would want to know if we'd held hands or kissed, or done anything else.

But maybe this might be love, talking about things that matter and saying how you really feel, instead of putting on a front to make people think everything's great when it's not.

As we turned the corner back towards Pizza Paradise his hand brushed accidentally against mine. Or was it accidental? Should I do anything or should I do nothing? I stared straight ahead. The conversation died away.

After a few seconds Kev took my hand hesitantly. We walked back slowly in silence. I was filled with happiness.

*　　*　　*

When we got back most of the crowd had gone. Deirdre and Andy were sitting talking, or rather Andy was holding forth and Deirdre was gazing at him. She told us the others had gone to a disco in the Sports Club in Ballytymon.

'Did Ruth go too?' I asked.

'Yeah, Bernie had to babysit, but Ruth and Therese went with the lads,' she said. 'Ruth had to ring home first. I heard her telling her mum that her headache was gone and her appendix had stopped grumbling.' We giggled.

Kev went up to the counter and got chips for us all. Deirdre put some money in the video jukebox and we sat down at the table talking and munching chips and watching Madonna.

Suddenly I felt a cold draught as the door of Pizza Paradise opened wide. In the doorway stood an amazing-looking girl. She was like a model, tall and thin, with very short spiky red hair and huge dangling gold earrings. She was wearing a tiny black mini-skirt, a bright yellow jacket and loads of make-up.

Everyone in the place was staring at her.

She looked round grimly and marched over to us, wobbling slightly on very high heels. Everything went quiet. Ignoring the rest of us, she addressed Kev loudly.

'And where the hell were you tonight, lover boy?'

The Scene

I don't think I'll ever forget what I afterwards came to think of as The Scene.

When the girl spoke, Kev, who was sitting beside me, looked away. After a few seconds he muttered, 'We weren't supposed to be doin' anything tonight.'

I had a sinking feeling. It had never occurred to me that he might already have a girlfriend. Even if it had, I would never have imagined anyone like her.

She was white with anger under her perfect make-up. She put her hands on her hips and said furiously, 'Listen Kev, we've been out together every bleedin' Saturday night for four months. And then you just shag off with your new snobby friends. I s'pose Ballytymon's not good enough for you now.'

Kev stood up. He said grimly, 'You really piss me off, Sinead. You're the one who wanted to break up. And it wasn't every Saturday, it was only when you'd nothing better on.'

She turned to me and said savagely, 'I s'pose you're the new love of his life. But you'll see, he'll chuck you too when it suits him.'

All eyes were now on me. My mind went blank as usual. I felt as if I was in a film and no-one had given me the script.

In the silence that followed Andy spoke up. 'Come off it, Sinead,' he said easily. 'You've been out with all of us on Saturday nights. Stop showing off. You're not a film star yet.'

'Get lost, Andy,' she snapped back.

But what he said seemed to deflate her. She glared at us all, and hissed at me, 'You'll be sorry,' just like the wicked witch in a fairy story. Then she stalked out.

Gradually people started talking again. I was near tears. Kev might have warned me about her, even if they had broken up. I looked at him. His face was like thunder.

Deirdre put her arm round me and whispered, 'D'you want to go?'

I nodded. We all filed out silently, watched by everyone in the place.

Deirdre and Andy chatted rather too brightly as we walked home. I tried to respond, but inside I felt hurt and humiliated. Kev didn't say a word. All the barriers were up and I felt we'd never again be able to talk frankly as we had in that magic hour which now seemed so long ago.

At the top of my road he said, unsmiling, 'See ya,' and went off with Andy to get the bus. Deirdre and I looked at each other.

'Well, he's sure got hidden depths,' she said, with new respect. 'Did you see her make-up? She must have had three different colours of eye shadow and loads of eyeliner and mascara. And her heels.' And that hair, I thought.

'Maybe I should ask for advice from "Dear Anne",' I said, 'it's just the sort of thing people write in about.' But I suspected that reading about situations like this in magazines is quite different from being involved in them yourself.

'Who needs "Dear Anne" when you've got me?' said Deirdre. 'I'll give you a ring tomorrow and we'll talk it over.' She sounded quite enthusiastic.

* * *

The light was on in the study when I came in and I guessed Dad must be working late as usual. His job has something to do with finance and he brings lots of files home with him.

Mum was watching 'Kenny Live' on TV. She came out of the living-room as soon as she heard my key in the lock. I steeled myself for questions. But although she looked as neat as ever, she appeared distracted.

'Did you have a nice time, Jackie? You were out with Deirdre and Ruth, weren't you?' she asked.

I opened my mouth, but before I could answer she announced, 'Your dad and I are going to Galway next weekend to stay with Auntie Gemma. She hasn't been well.' She must mean the hysterectomy I wasn't supposed to know about.

She went on. 'And we could do with a break, especially Dad. He's very tired, and he's got a lot on his mind.'

I was vaguely aware that Dad had been even quieter than usual recently. I'd even mentioned it to Kev. Perhaps Mum was right and he was tired.

But I couldn't help remembering the row I'd overheard the previous week. Late at night I'd been woken by raised voices from downstairs. My parents didn't argue much and when Dad did shout it was usually at Philip because he was being really annoying.

I'd crept out onto the landing and found Philip sitting in his pyjamas at the top of the stairs. We listened for a bit. The argument seemed to be about money. A small needle of anxiety stirred inside me.

Even Philip was subdued, but only for a moment. 'I hope they're still getting me the new racer for my birthday,' he whispered.

'Honestly, Philip, how selfish can you be?' I muttered. 'They must have some money problems.' I thought of Kev and Bernie and their mother. I shivered.

'Well, Mum promised,' he answered, aggrieved. 'I'll be twelve, and Sean's had one since last year. He can even drive his brother's car sometimes.' Sean is Philip's friend. My parents think he's a bad influence. His family's really well-off and his older brother, who's only twenty, owns a car, a battered Fiat Panda.

'That's rubbish, Sean wouldn't be allowed drive,' I snapped. He stuck out his tongue in reply.

.

It had gone quiet downstairs and we both went back to bed. I'd forgotten all about the incident until now.

'You're not listening,' Mum was saying. With an effort I tried to concentrate. It had been a long day. She looked at me closely. 'You look exhausted, dear. Are you hungry? There's some tea brack in the tin.'

'Oh great,' I said brightly. Actually I was starving. I remembered Deirdre reading in *Teen Dreams* that stress could make you crave food.

Mum followed me into the kitchen. 'Nana has offered to come and stay while we're in Galway.'

I groaned. 'Mum, I'm almost sixteen.' Well, I would be in another few months. 'I don't need anyone to mind me.'

'Well, Philip does,' said Mum. I couldn't argue with that.

'Couldn't we have Gran instead? She's not so cross.'

'No, Gran's not really able for it any more. It's very good of Nana. She'll be missing one of her bridge nights. It's no picnic minding Philip,' she said with a sigh. I knew what she meant all right.

'I'm counting on you to give her a hand, Jackie,' she added.

I wondered if I should tell her about Kev. But there wasn't much point if it was all over between us. And I couldn't face describing The Scene.

Instead I said abruptly, 'Is there something wrong with Dad?'

She said quickly, 'No, of course not. He's just got a few problems at work. Nothing for you to worry about.' But she was frowning as she left the kitchen. Maybe I ought to try and cheer her up.

'Your hair looks nice,' I called after her. 'Did you get the highlights touched up?'

She reappeared in the doorway. 'Yesterday,' she said. 'Nana said she would bring me personally to Marcel if I didn't.' She smiled and went up to bed. I attacked the tea brack.

* * *

In bed that night my thoughts turned back to Kev and Sinead and The Scene.

What should I do next? Surely it was up to him to get in touch? He'd certainly been raging. But was it with her or me or both? Or himself? And shouldn't I be the one to be raging? The small problems I had mentioned to Kev seemed to be growing bigger by the minute.

I tossed and turned restlessly for what seemed like hours, and when I finally got to sleep I had confused dreams about Sinead and Kev.

I woke up feeling as exhausted as if I had spent the night training for the marathon.

* * *

I was still thinking about The Scene the following week while we were watching a school hockey match. Therese and Deirdre were in the team and the rest of us were shivering dutifully in an icy wind on the sidelines.

Afterwards we went to have coffee in the shopping centre. I knew what the chief topic was going to be. Everyone had an opinion on how to handle the situation.

'You've got to assert yourself,' said Therese firmly. 'I'll find out where Sinead lives and we'll go round and tell her to lay off you and Kev.'

'That's no good,' argued Deirdre, munching a doughnut. 'Jackie'll have to talk it over calmly and constructively with Kev and Sinead.'

Ruth watched disapprovingly as Deirdre licked her fingers and Therese and I each took a chocolate biscuit. 'All those things are full of sugar and additives –,' she began.

'Honestly, Ruth, health is all you think about. What about Jackie's problems?' said Deirdre accusingly. Ruth looked hurt.

'I know,' I said suddenly, 'I'll talk to Bernie.' None of them was too pleased with this idea.

'Well, of course, if you don't want to listen to your best friends.' Deirdre was in a huff.

'Look, she's Kev's sister, she'll know the whole story.' Then I remembered Andy's intervention that night. He must know the story too.

'Has Andy said anything?' I asked Deirdre.

'I haven't heard from him,' she admitted after a pause.

Therese put down her mug and thumped the table. 'This stupid waiting for fellas to phone has got to stop. Why don't you phone them for a change?'

'They're not on the phone,' snapped Deirdre.

'You could get Kev at Burgerama, couldn't you?' Therese countered, turning to me. 'Why can't you phone him there?'

I stood up. I'd had enough advice for one day. 'I'm going home,' I announced firmly. 'I still haven't finished the Romantic poets and we've got to hand it in tomorrow.'

The others picked up their bags and followed. Maybe there is something to be said for asserting yourself.

The Heart to Heart

Sitting in the bus as we jolted from stop to stop on the way home from school I stared blindly at the bright springtime gardens. I was wondering how to contact Bernie.

Therese, beside me, was grumbling about the brutal maths homework which she was sure was going to take all night. 'My brother's getting the video of *The Snapper* and I'm dying to see it,' she moaned.

The others had gone to the Woodgrove Centre to look for a leather jacket for Deirdre. Her parents were getting her one for her birthday. It had been the main topic of conversation until it was replaced by my love life.

Despite everyone's advice I was convinced I needed Bernie's help. After all, she knew Kev better than anyone.

But I could see I'd have to be careful not to hurt Deirdre's feelings. She is my best friend. Mum is always telling me how important good friends are. Dad thinks that they should be 'the right type of friends', whatever that means.

I think it should mean the ones you can rely on when things go wrong. But I'm not sure if that's what Dad means.

*   *   *

The wind had dropped and the evening was still and cool. As I walked up our road I could see my brother careering around on the back of his friend Sean's racer. As soon as they saw me they started shouting insults.

Unluckily for them Mum was in the front porch planting geraniums in pots. She straightened up.

'Stop that now,' she told them sharply. She looked at Sean who was pedalling wildly and waving his hands above his head. 'Isn't it time you went home, Sean? Surely you've got homework?'

'We didn't get any, our teacher's sick,' said Sean.

I'm not surprised, I thought, so would I be if I had to teach them. For Mum's sake I left the thought unsaid.

'Can Philip come to my house?' asked Sean. 'He wants to see my brother's car.'

'Not now, Sean. Philip's room's a disgrace, he'll have to go and tidy it.' I hoped she hadn't looked in my room.

Mum turned to me. 'Jackie, someone called Bernie phoned for you. She said she'd ring back. She sounded nice, is she from your school?'

'No, I met her at the disco in Ballytymon. She lives near Therese. We all got friendly with her and her brother.' At last I'd mentioned Kev to her.

'From Ballytymon?' repeated my mother anxiously.

'What sort of a home do they come from?'

'You said she sounded nice. Well, she is,' I replied coldly. 'What difference does it make where their home is, it's what people are like that counts, isn't it? They're certainly nicer than some people I know.' I looked pointedly at Philip who was aiming kicks at the neat clumps of flowers beside the front porch.

'All right, all right,' said Mum. 'You can't be too careful these days. You'll understand when you have children of your own.'

'Well, I won't make remarks about their friends when I don't even know them,' I said under my breath as I marched into the house.

'What did you say, dear?' Mum said absently, her attention distracted by Philip's assault on the daffodils.

'Nothing.' I felt really fed up.

As I went in the phone was ringing. It was Bernie.

'Bernie,' I said joyfully, 'am I glad to hear from you.' I wondered if she'd heard about the famous Scene. It wasn't going to be easy trying to describe it over the phone, especially with Mum and Philip around.

I went on, 'Listen, I need to talk to you. Can you come over after school tomorrow?'

'I could come on Thursday,' she said. I felt instantly soothed by her calm tone. Then she added, 'Look, don't worry about Sinead. I'll explain when I see you. Kev doesn't really like her.'

My heart jumped. I realised that I'd missed the up and

down feelings. Recently it had all been down.

'What did he say?' I asked.

'He didn't say much. But I know he's pissed off.'

'It's hard to get through to him, isn't it? To know how he feels inside?' I thought sadly of the one time I had got through to him.

I could hear screams in the background. 'I'd better go,' said Bernie. 'There's a queue for the phone, and Sharon's dropped her Big Dipper and it's gone all down her Batman T-shirt. See you Thursday.'

Dragging my bag I went slowly up the stairs and put U2 on at full blast. I got out *Français Aujourd'hui* and turned to my portrait gallery in the back. Choosing a black marker I dashed off a vicious cartoon of Sinead, with long talons for nails and eyes dripping with make-up. 'That'll teach you to call me snobby, stupid cow,' I muttered.

Then I noticed the picture I'd done of Kev before we'd met, when there'd only been The Look. Everything had been easier when he'd just been a sort of dream. Now that he was a real person it was all much more complicated.

I felt so confused about him. I remembered the glow of happiness when we walked back to Pizza Paradise holding hands. I had never felt like that before.

But I couldn't forget his grim expression after The Scene, or what Sinead said about him chucking me if it suited him.

Would I ever find out which was the real Kev? Or would he always be a mystery man?

I got out the Romantic poets. Maybe they were the closest I was ever going to get to romance.

* * *

I could see that despite her doubts Mum was impressed by Bernie.

She had just got back from doing Meals on Wheels, and she came into the hall as Bernie and I were going upstairs with a couple of Cokes from the fridge.

'Mum, this is Bernie,' I said uneasily, remembering the argument we'd had.

Bernie was wearing the navy cotton sweater that set off her shining hair so well, and black Levi's. She smiled politely at my mother.

'Would you like something to eat, girls?'

'No, I'm grand, thanks,' replied Bernie. I could almost hear Mum thinking what good manners she had.

We hurried upstairs.

'Your ma's cool,' said Bernie. I thought of Mum's earlier comments but said nothing.

Bernie looked admiringly at my collection of cuddly animals. 'They're sweet,' she said. 'The kids have robbed all of my old toys.'

'What ages are the kids?' I asked her.

'Lisa's ten, and Fiona and Sharon are seven and nearly five. They're little terrors,' she said. 'You must come round. You'll need ear plugs.'

She sat beside me on the bed among the heaps of

clothes. 'I can't stay long,' she said. 'I heard about the other night. I thought you'd want to know about Sinead. I suppose Kev told you nothing?'

'No, but Andy made it sound as though they'd known her for ages.'

'We've all known her for ages, she lives near us. She was all right until she started drama classes and then she kind of went off her head.' Bernie tucked her feet under her on the bed and leant against my giant panda, won by Gran in a raffle.

She went on, 'She thinks she's great, though everyone else thinks she's a bit thick. And she's always putting on a show.'

'So that's why Andy told her she wasn't a film star yet?'

'Yeah,' said Bernie. I opened another Coke.

'And that night in Pizza Paradise, she was doing the big star act?'

'Yeah, except you didn't even know there was a show, or that you were in it.' She grinned and we both started giggling. Suddenly it didn't seem to matter so much, it was even something to laugh about.

'Mind you,' Bernie went on, 'she does look cool, even with all that make-up. My mum knows her aunt and she says it takes her at least an hour to put it all on. She works in a boutique in the new shopping centre in Ballytymon and they say she gets all her clothes half price. That's why she looks like a model.'

I thought to myself in my usual negative way that even

if I got all my clothes for nothing I would never look like a model.

Aloud I said, 'I suppose all the lads are after her?'

'She's been out with most of them but it never lasts because she's always looking for someone better. She can be a real cow.' I knew that all right.

'And Kev?'

'He went out with her for a bit. I think she went for him 'cos he can play the guitar.'

Did they hold hands, I wondered. Or anything else? And Kev had never even mentioned the guitar to me. I felt a familiar stab.

'I didn't like what she said about us being your new snobby friends.'

Bernie looked at me with a serious expression. For a moment she reminded me of Kev. 'Don't mind her. She's just jealous,' she said.

Well I certainly knew about feeling jealous, I thought, though I'd never imagined anyone being jealous of me.

Bernie went on, 'Even if we live in different places we can still be friends. I don't think you or the others are snobby. And Kev doesn't either.'

I felt a sense of relief, as if a weight had been lifted off my shoulders. But there was one more thing.

'Why hasn't Kev got in touch? Are we going to see each other again or is that it?' I hoped I didn't sound too dramatic, like Sinead.

Bernie stood up and smiled gently. 'I think he needs

space. He's a bit mixed up. And he's raging about Dad going off and everything.'

At the door she said, 'He told me he could've murdered Sinead. He thinks you're different from other girls.'

* * *

After waving Bernie off I went in to watch 'Home and Away'. Maybe Kev was raging, like Bernie said, but Sinead is so glamorous and I look so ordinary and my hair is such a mess. And whenever I'm with him I can hardly ever think of anything to say. I mean, 'different from other girls' isn't the greatest compliment you could get.

Stop this, I told myself. Therese is always telling me to be positive and assertive. But it's not so easy, especially with a pretty friend like Deirdre, and a moody boyfriend like Kev, and a glam rival like Sinead.

I slumped down into the armchair. Philip came in from the garden and stretched out on the rug. We usually call a truce while 'Home and Away' is on.

Maybe I should try to forget about Kev. Maybe it's not love after all.

The Reconciliation

He was waiting when I came out of school the next day. It was the start of the mid-term break and we had a half-day. Bernie must have found out from Therese and told him. He was standing at the corner wearing a dark blue sweatshirt and jeans. He looked up as we approached and smiled straight at me.

My heart lurched and I had to stop for a moment. So much for trying to forget about him, I thought.

As the others walked ahead tactfully, Therese whispered, 'Remember you're a woman and not a mouse.' As advice it wasn't a great help. And neither was the fact that I was wearing my turquoise uniform again.

Everyone headed off down the road, but Kev and I gradually fell behind. As soon as the others were out of sight round the bend he took my hand quite confidently. Maybe he'd had advice from the lads like I had from my crowd.

'Look,' he said immediately, as if he'd been rehearsing,

'Sorry about the other night. Sinead's just trying to stir things up. I meant to ring you.'

'Bernie came to the rescue,' I said.

'As usual,' he said wryly. 'Anyway let's forget it. I don't have to be in work till five. Want to go for a walk?'

It felt so great just to be walking along with him that I couldn't bring myself to ask questions. There was quite a lot more I wanted to know about him and Sinead, but he'd dismissed it all so firmly. I'd have to wait for some other opportunity. Deirdre and her agony columns would be proud of me, I thought. But Therese and her assertiveness wouldn't. There's just no way to please them all and Kev too.

* * *

We caught up with the others at the bus stop. The bus came almost immediately and we all piled on and rushed up the stairs.

The others were laughing and shrieking at the tops of their voices. Kev and I followed more quietly.

'I'm wrecked,' said Ruth flopping into a seat. 'I'm not going to do a tap the whole weekend.'

'Yeah, everyone's noticed how overworked you are,' Deirdre said sarcastically. Ruth usually finishes off her weekend homework on the bus on Monday mornings.

'McCabe's given us a massive commerce project for the mid-term break,' groaned Therese.

'*Mr* McCabe to you, Therese,' Deirdre said, in Miss Kinsella's sharp tone.

'He's your typical male chauvinist,' said Therese. 'He's just working out his aggression on us 'cos we're female.' Kev looked uncomfortable.

Fortunately Ruth changed the subject. 'I think I might have a dose of the flu coming on,' she complained. 'I can feel a tickle in my throat.' Everyone groaned.

An inspector appeared, whistling as he climbed the stairs. He knew we were regulars. 'Off early again?' he said cheerily. 'You lot never do a tap in that school.' He grinned at the chorus of protests.

We waved our passes at him. When he got to Kev he stopped. 'You with this lot?' he asked, jerking his head at us. Kev nodded uneasily.

'Well, you'd better look out for all these young wans, they're a danger.' He winked at Kev.

'Another male chauvinist,' Therese said to Deirdre in a deafening whisper. Why did the conversation keep coming round to male chauvinists just when Kev was there? I threw Deirdre an appealing glance.

She came over to where I was sitting with Kev and said brightly, 'Hey Jackie, if you're going off with Kev I'll take your bag home. You can collect it later.'

'Thanks a million,' I said. She turned to Kev and said casually, 'What's Andy up to these days?'

'He's doing late nights in Dunnes,' he answered after a moment's hesitation. 'I'll tell him you were asking for him.'

'Don't bother,' Deirdre said rather snappily. 'I'm going out with Mark tomorrow.'

It was the first I knew of it. I felt guilty for having been so wrapped up in my own problems. I could see that Andy was fun, but he never let you forget he thought he was the greatest. On the other hand he was certainly more interesting than Mark, who was very serious and mostly talked about computers.

'I'll call round later, Deirdre,' I said. And I must remember to ask her the latest on Mark and Andy, I told myself.

She staggered as she took my bag. 'What've you got in here, the kitchen sink?'

I always take home all my books on holidays in the usually vain hope that having them there might encourage me to study.

*   *   *

Kev and I got off the bus at Rathnure and turned into the park. There were loads of little kids in buggies or on tricycles, mostly with mothers, some with dads. Everyone looked cheerful in the sunshine.

We walked down the slope into the woods. Everywhere there were tiny new green leaves and pink blossom. We strolled along the grassy path, holding hands. I thought about all the times I'd looked enviously at a fella and girl hand-in-hand in the park in spring, and wished I was that girl. And now I was. It was really worth all the hassle.

For once the conversation flowed easily. In fact we talked about everything except Sinead.

At the lake we stopped to watch a row of baby ducks

swimming jerkily behind their mother.

'I wish we had some bread,' I said, as we watched two little kids wildly flinging crusts in all directions while their mothers sat chatting on a bench. None of the bread went anywhere near the ducks.

The mention of food made us hungry. Kev produced a Double Decker from his pocket and we ate half each.

'Bernie told me you play the guitar,' I said. I didn't tell him that Bernie thought his guitar was what had impressed Sinead.

'Yeah, I play lead in a group. We do some gigs in Ballytymon. Andy's on the drums.' He added, 'If you can sing, we need a girl vocal.'

'I'd be hopeless,' I laughed, pleased to be asked. I just hoped Sinead couldn't sing either.

* * *

When we arrived at the swings a crowd of screaming kids were having a go on the see-saw, crashing it up and down violently. I saw with relief that none of them was Philip. It's just the sort of thing he'd be up to.

Kev and I each sat on one of the swings. Thinking of Therese, I finally nerved myself to ask him the important question. Trying to sound casual I said, 'Have you and Sinead really broken up?' I had a bit of trouble saying her name.

He didn't reply straight away and I could see he was frowning. At last he spoke. 'Yeah, we'd both had enough.

But you never know with Sinead. You saw yourself what she's like.'

We walked on in silence. It wasn't a very satisfactory answer. Did this mean whenever Sinead decided to make a scene Kev was going to disappear in a huff?

Therese had said only yesterday, when we were discussing the subject yet again, that Kev was just stringing me along and I ought to drop him. But a boyfriend isn't easy to find, at least not for me. Especially one who makes your heart jump.

Anyway, surely assertiveness means doing what you want to do yourself, not just what someone else thinks you should. And my instinct is to do what Bernic says, give Kev some space.

On the other hand, I assured Therese silently, I'm not going to wait around for ever and be hassled by Sinead while he makes up his mind.

We wandered on, hands clasped, my mind seething with conflicting thoughts. Why is everything so simple in stories and films and so difficult in real life?

Kev cleared his throat nervously and looked at me. 'I like your hair.'

I stared at him in disbelief. I hadn't even had time to put mousse on it this morning, or the extra shine hairspray. Then I thought, could this be his way of saying he cares about me, like I do sometimes with Mum?

He reached out and touched my hair awkwardly. A warm glow spread slowly through me. He put his arm round me and we walked back through the park towards my house. At least he walked, and I sort of floated.

The Kiss

When we got home I debated whether to bring Kev in. Mum was now quite a fan of Bernie's, but I wasn't sure how she would feel about Kev.

As we sat on the wall in front of the house, I was surprised to see Dad's car draw up. He was never home this early. Then I remembered that they were going to Galway for the weekend.

Dad got out carrying a load of files and his briefcase. He said, 'Hello, Jackie,' nodded vaguely to Kev and went inside.

A few minutes later my mother appeared. 'Mum,' I said, 'this is Kev, he's Bernie's brother.'

'Hi,' mumbled Kev.

She gave him a brief nod and turned to me. 'Jackie, I want to tell you about the food for the weekend. And you'd better be here when Philip gets back. Nana's got a headache already and we haven't even left yet.'

Kev and I could both see that Mum was in a state. It

wasn't the best time for a social visit.

Kev said, 'See ya,' and went off.

*   *   *

I followed Mum into the hall which was full of bags and suitcases.

Dad came out of the study, took one look and said, 'It looks as if we're going on safari for a month, not Galway for a weekend.'

'Some of this is Nana's,' said Mum. 'She's brought enough with her for a month as well.'

Then the inevitable question came. Dad turned to me and asked casually, 'Who was that lad?'

'His name's Kev, he's just a friend.' I knew that wasn't going to be enough.

'Is he from Ballytymon?' Mum must have told him.

I had the feeling it was soon going to be time for a bit of assertiveness.

'I hope he's not mixed up with any of those joyriders,' said Dad, picking up a suitcase.

A cold angry feeling welled up inside me.

Mum chimed in quickly. 'Jackie brought home that boy's sister. She's seems a nice type of girl.' I looked at her, surprised to have support.

But the anger didn't go away. I addressed Dad furiously. 'It's not fair to say someone's a joyrider just because they live in Ballytymon. There are lots of people who rob cars who live all over the place, even Rathnure, I bet.'

Dad looked taken aback. 'I never meant –' he began.

I interrupted him. I didn't know where this torrent of words was coming from. I just couldn't stop. 'What about that man from our road who knocked a girl down in his car when he was drunk? I remember you saying he was no better than a murderer. But you wouldn't say everyone living in Rathnure is a drunken driver, just because he lives here.' I was amazed to hear myself making such an articulate speech. Maybe I should try debating in school. I'd always thought I'd be hopeless at it.

Dad was on the defensive. 'I didn't mean to suggest this boy is a joy-rider –'

'In fact he had to leave school and take a job to support his family,' I put in.

'– and if I did I'm sorry,' he finished, looking miserable. All the anger drained away and I suddenly felt sorry for him. On top of all his other problems he now had a furious daughter attacking him when he least expected it.

There was a loud bang on the front door. Mum opened it. Philip stood there, for once silenced by the sight of all three of us standing in the hall with strained expressions, surrounded by suitcases. He took a step back. 'I didn't do nothing,' he shouted.

There was a shuffling from the kitchen and Nana appeared wearing the pink furry slippers she always wore when she came to stay.

'What is going on?' she asked plaintively. 'It's so noisy and I've got a headache. Why is everyone shouting?'

Her eye fell on Philip. 'Philip, tuck your shirt in. And look at the state of your shoes.' She turned to me. 'Jackie, your hair. At least give it a brush.'

Philip and I exchanged glances, united by Nana's familiar complaints.

Dad grabbed two suitcases and loaded them into the car. Philip staggered up to the spare room with Nana's bags, which calmed her down a bit.

I followed Mum out to the car. I was glad I'd said what I had but I didn't really want them to go off after an argument without things being smoothed over.

'Have a good trip, give our love to Auntie Gemma and the kids. Don't worry about us,' I said, giving them both a kiss.

Mum looked relieved. 'You will be careful, dear, won't you? Help Nana with everything.'

'Keep an eye on Philip,' said Dad. He gave a rare smile. 'Don't let Nana bring you to the dreaded Marcel,' he added with a wink.

Mum got in and rolled down the window. 'I've left some money with Nana for emergencies. And if the garage rings about my car ask how much it will cost for the service. And don't forget to thaw the mince thoroughly –'

Dad hurriedly started the car. Standing at the door we all heaved sighs of relief as we finally waved them off.

* * *

Philip was sent up to do his homework, with dire warnings not to play any Heavy Metal, and I dutifully made Nana a

cup of tea, fetched her aspirin and her knitting and offered
to peel the potatoes.

As we pottered round the kitchen I noticed her looking
at me speculatively.

'What's wrong, Nana?' I asked. She gave me a winning
smile.

'Jackie dear, what about coming with me to Marcel
tomorrow morning? He'd do a lovely job. You won't know
yourself.'

I sighed. That was what I was afraid of. My hair may
not be great, but it's the way I am. I don't think I suddenly
want to look like someone else, certainly not Nana.

I said, 'Thanks anyway, Nana, but I think I'll leave it as
it is for now,' trying to sound polite but firm. I hoped it
wasn't going to be the main topic of the weekend.

*   *   *

Friday and Saturday were punctuated by phonecalls from
Mum in Galway and Gran in Dublin, plus several visits
from neighbours. Mum must have arranged for a rota of
people to check on us.

Nana got a bit fed up when the second well-meaning
neighbour called just as she was putting her feet up after
lunch. 'You must have a very good Neighbourhood Watch
scheme here,' she said sharply to the visitor who beat a
hasty retreat.

Philip had been unusually quiet and well-behaved since
Mum and Dad left. Nana was sure it was her magic touch.

I hoped he wasn't up to something.

After tea on Saturday he went round to Sean's house with strict instructions to be back by half nine. I was due to babysit for the Nolans, who lived round the corner. Deirdre was meeting Mark later but said she'd come for a while and keep me company. Kev had said he'd come to the Nolans' house after he finished work around ten.

I knew the Nolans wouldn't mind people calling in to see me. They were really cool, although their four-year-old twins could be terrors.

I went up and put on my fancy leggings and borrowed Mum's black silky blouse and a squirt of her good perfume, Eternity. I hoped she wouldn't mind.

When I came down I looked in on Nana who was sitting in the armchair with her knitting on her lap, watching 'Blind Date'. She jumped when I came in. 'Just waiting for the wildlife programme,' she said, picking up her knitting. She sounded guilty because she always said that most TV programmes were rubbish except Gay Byrne, Bibi Baskin, wildlife and the news.

Before I could say anything she said quickly, 'Don't forget your key, dear. You know I like to go to bed early.'

At least being caught out watching 'Blind Date' had taken her mind off my hair. She hadn't even looked at it. I closed the front door quietly.

* * *

'Well, what's with Kev these days?' Deirdre asked encouragingly as we sat in front of the TV dipping into a box of chocolates left for me by Mrs Nolan, and resolutely closing our ears to muffled thumps from the twins' bedroom above.

I had already heard the latest episode in the search for the ultimate leather jacket which had been going on for the last two months. I sometimes despaired of Deirdre ever finding the right one.

Then I reminded myself it was about time I took more of an interest in Deirdre's love life instead of dwelling on my own.

'First, what's the latest on Andy and Mark?' I asked her. I couldn't help my thoughts drifting though, as she launched into a comparison of their good and bad points.

'– the thing is, I realise Mark's steady and reliable, but I'm not really looking forward much to seeing him tonight. All that talk about computers gives me a pain. Andy always makes me laugh, but you never know –'

We were interrupted by one of the twins bursting into the room in his Aladdin pyjamas, his chubby cheeks scarlet with rage.

'Jackie! Jackie! She frew my soover in de loo,' he roared when he could draw breath.

We dashed upstairs, and by the time we had fished out the soother and washed it, sorted out the mess and pacified the twins and put them back in their bunk beds it was time for Deirdre to leave.

It was blissfully quiet when Kev arrived, late as usual. At least Sinead won't turn up here, I thought, although I wouldn't put it past her to find out where I babysit. I told myself not to get neurotic about her.

Kev said Bernie was minding the kids. Their mum's nerves were bad and she'd gone to bed.

I said hesitantly, 'It must be tough for Bernie, with your mum being sick and that.'

He looked angry. 'Yeah, that's what my dad's done for us. She wouldn't be sick only for him.'

I was always a bit scared by Kev's bitterness towards his dad. I mean, I was often fed up with Mum or Dad about something, but I couldn't imagine feeling as Kev did. But then we'd never been deserted like Kev and Bernie and their mum.

I wanted to change the subject but my mind blanked out as usual.

Then Kev said, 'Maybe some night when I'm off work we could mind the kids and let Bernie go out.'

'Yeah,' I said with mixed feelings. I was relieved that he'd cheered up, and that he was talking about future times together for us, and I wanted to help Bernie.

But I was a bit uptight at the thought of going to his house and meeting his mother. And his sisters sounded a bit of a handful. And what about Mum and Dad?

Be positive, I told myself. Surely with my experience of the Nolan twins and a brother like Philip, coping with any other kids would be child's play. And I reckoned Dad had seen my side for once in the argument we'd had about Kev.

We sat on the couch munching chocolates in the warmth of the fire. I put on a video – *Mrs Doubtfire* – but I was so aware of Kev beside me that I couldn't concentrate, even on the funny bits.

Then, after what seemed like an age, Kev put his arm round me. I sat very still, wondering what I should be doing. I thought of Deirdre and the 'Dear Anne' column. Where was all the advice now when I really needed it? I had a vague recollection that you were supposed to relax. I tried, but it's not easy when you're all wound up.

Finally we kissed, a bit clumsily due to lack of practice, at least on my part. Kev seemed quite awkward too and at first I felt tense and anxious. I could feel his heart thumping and realised he was as nervous as I was.

I did relax then, and the glow of warmth and sweetness that I had felt before surged through me. I didn't know a boy's lips would be so soft.

As we sat in front of the fire, the TV flickering, Kev's arm round me, I thought, at last, I'm really certain, this *must* be love.

*   *   *

The Nolans didn't seem to mind Kev being there when they got back. When Mrs Nolan called me into the kitchen to pay me she said smiling, 'He looks a nice boy.'

No-one mentioned that we had finished almost an entire box of chocolates in the course of the evening. And in return I didn't tell them about the twins' soother being thrown in the loo.

As Kev walked me home through a soft drizzle I thought, for the first time everything's going right with Kev and me, the usual problems don't seem to matter any more.

That was until we rounded the corner and saw the squad car, lights flashing and engine running, right outside my house.

The Crime

As I rushed through the open front door, followed more slowly by Kev, a weird sight met my eyes.

The hall was full of people all talking at once. It was like a scene in a play. Nana stood at the foot of the stairs wearing a violent pink dressing-gown and her furry slippers, her hair done up in rollers and a hairnet, her skin shining with night cream.

Facing her were two huge uniformed gardaí. One had his hand firmly on Philip's shoulder. Philip was filthy, his grubby shirt hanging out and one shoe missing. He was crying quietly, the tears making two tracks down his grimy cheeks. Sean, Philip's friend, stood beside him looking defiant.

As we burst in everyone stopped talking and turned to look at us as though we'd just arrived from Mars.

'What's happened?' My voice sounded squeaky.

The guard holding Philip said, 'Are you the sister?' I nodded, feeling my stomach knotting up with fright. Philip gave a loud sob and sniff.

The guard took out a notebook, glanced at it and fixed his eyes on me. 'We're investigating a serious situation,' he said heavily. 'Two lads were driving a vehicle illegally and caused damage to property. Our information is that these are the two. We'll need to speak to the parents.'

My voice shook. 'They're away in Galway.'

The guard looked at Kev. 'Who's this?'

'He's just a friend,' I said quickly. I could see Nana eyeing Kev suspiciously.

'Whose car was it?' I asked.

We all looked at Philip and Sean. Philip gave another loud sniff. Sean wore his usual cocky look, but when he opened his mouth nothing came out. It was the first time I'd ever seen him silenced.

The guard let go of Philip and turned over a page of his notebook. 'They appear to have taken a Fiat Panda car, registration number SZV 59, the property of a Mr Donal Byrne.' That was Sean's elder brother. He went on, 'They drove the vehicle some distance in an erratic fashion, damaged two parked cars and a lamp-post, and then abandoned it. They ran away and were followed by a garda car and apprehended outside this house.'

There was a shocked silence and another sniff from Philip.

Nana sank down on to the stairs. She said feebly, 'What'll your dad say when he hears this? And your poor mother?'

At this Philip sobbed loudly. He was such a pathetic

sight that I put my arm round him. Near tears myself I turned to Kev. He touched my shoulder awkwardly, looking as if he'd rather be somewhere else.

The other guard addressed me. 'You'd better contact your parents. They should come to Rathnure Garda Station tomorrow with the lad to make a statement.'

Nana said, 'This is all because Philip's got into bad company.' She pointed to Sean. 'He's the cause of the trouble.'

'No, it was Philip, it was his fault.' Sean had found his voice, but it sounded hoarse.

Philip stopped sniffing and muttered, 'Sean said his brother wouldn't mind if we went up the road in the car to get chips.'

'We're going round to this lad's house now,' the guard told Nana. Sean's bold front collapsed at this and he gulped. 'My dad'll kill me,' he quavered.

'Not before time,' said Nana sharply. She'd clearly decided where the blame lay.

One of the guards said quietly, 'There's two of them in it, ma'am.' With a muttered goodnight they marched out with Sean, looking very small, shuffling between them.

Kev said, with a glance at Nana, 'I'll be off.' I wished he could stay and give me some much needed moral support but I could see it wasn't on. I followed him out of the front door.

Outside Kev turned and looked at me with his serious look. I remembered the kiss. It was only an hour ago but it seemed like a lifetime. I had that funny feeling in my nose you get when you're going to cry. He put his arm round me. I felt his cheek touch my hair. A sense of comfort and closeness filled me. Then he was gone.

I took a deep breath and went back inside. I felt better. I wasn't going to cry, I was going to take charge.

'I think we'll have a cup of tea,' I said firmly to Nana and Philip, who were both sniffling. 'And then I'll phone Dad.'

I led the way to the kitchen.

*   *   *

Both Mum and Dad were in a state of shock when they got back on Sunday morning. Nana met them at the door with a tearful rambling version of the story.

When we were sitting round the kitchen table with cups of tea in front of us, Philip was made to give an account of what had happened.

Apparently Sean had insisted that his brother wouldn't mind them using his car. Sean had taken the keys and done the driving. They'd headed for the nearby chipper.

When they grazed a couple of parked cars the boys had panicked and veered into a lamp-post at the end of Sean's road. They'd both jumped out and run away.

The guards must have been called by neighbours who heard the bang. When Philip and Sean heard the police siren they had tried to hide in the garden, not very successfully.

Dad shook his head. 'They could have killed someone.'

'Or been killed,' added my mother, lifting her cup with a shaking hand.

'I blame myself,' Dad went on. 'I should be here more, give him some attention. But with the trouble at work –' He stopped.

I was going to ask, 'What trouble?' but Nana interrupted. 'Maybe I'm just not able for minding the children any more.'

'It wasn't your fault,' said Mum. 'Perhaps we shouldn't have gone to Galway.' She looked at Dad.

Nana went on, 'The shame of such a thing in our family. I just hope Sylvia and Maureen don't hear about it.'

* * *

'You'd think your Nana would be more worried about what'll happen to Philip,' said Deirdre when I recounted the weekend's drama on the bus on Monday morning.

'That's what Dad said. He told her she had her priorities wrong, and she was too concerned about the opinions of Sylvia and Maureen. They're her bridge partners,' I explained to Deirdre. 'Then Nana said Philip was spoilt and Mum burst into tears. Then Philip started bawling. I had to make tea for everyone again.' I sighed. 'I never thought it could be a relief to come to school.'

'Poor thing,' said Deirdre sympathetically as we gathered up our bags. 'What about Sean?'

'His brother's raging about the damage to his car. I don't think it's covered by insurance.'

We jumped off the bus and walked slowly towards school. 'Mum says all the children in Sean's family have everything too easy,' I told Deirdre.

'Oh yeah, my dad's always going on about things coming too easy,' said Deirdre. 'I had to wait a year before they'd agree to get me the leather jacket, and I have to save half the money myself.'

And we swung into the leather jacket conversation. I was quite glad to get off the subject of Philip and Sean and what was beginning to feel like the Crime of the Century.

* * *

But later, in English class, my thoughts kept returning to the subject. We were reading through *Hamlet* and I was the ghost of Hamlet's father, who fortunately didn't have much more to say.

I had found, as that endless Sunday dragged on, punctuated by tears, anxious whispered exchanges and yet more tea, that in their shock and distress both Mum and Dad seemed to turn to me for support. Somehow we were able to talk more freely than usual.

'I just can't believe this is happening,' Mum kept saying, after they came back from the Garda Station with Philip, all of them looking pale and drawn.

'Perhaps it'll turn out for the best,' Dad said, patting her shoulder comfortingly. I had a sudden memory of Kev doing the same to me. 'It's given him a fright and shaken us up too,' he went on. 'Maybe we needed that, at least I did.'

They seemed to know about Kev having been with me that evening. Nana must have told them. I'd hoped she'd forgotten in all the excitement.

But Dad only said, 'It's just as well you weren't on your own when you came back and found the guards here. It must have been quite an ordeal. I'm proud of the way you handled it.'

I thought back to the row we'd had about Kev, and the remarks he'd made about joy-riders. It seemed ages ago now, almost as though it had happened in another life.

I was thinking all this over during English class, when I gradually became aware of an expectant silence.

I looked up. Miss Kinsella's eyes were on me, and Therese beside me was signalling desperately and whispering what sounded like 'Swear, swear.' What could she mean?

Then my eye fell on the copy of *Hamlet* on the desk in front of me. It said, 'Ghost: Swear.'

'Swear,' I said at last in a quavering voice. There were suppressed giggles.

'I suppose the long pause was meant to make it sound more dramatic, Jackie,' said Miss Kinsella sarcastically at the end of the scene. 'I'm glad you're so absorbed by the play. We'll have to give you a bigger part in future.'

I turned my attention from Philip to *Hamlet*.

The Initiative

I n school the next day I made up my mind to go to Burgerama and see if Kev was there. I hadn't heard from him or Bernie since the night of The Crime.

Although I'd told Deirdre about what had happened, I hadn't said much to the others. They'd obviously heard about it from her, but they were being tactful and not saying much to me.

The person I wanted to talk to most was Kev. I was sure he and Bernie would understand in a way the others might not. And even through all the hassle with Philip the memory of kissing Kev, and of how I'd felt, still lingered.

As usual I'd been waiting for him to get in touch, but I was beginning to accept that he was always slow to make a move, and if I wanted to keep the relationship going I'd have to make the running myself instead of agonising.

Maybe all the talk about assertiveness was having an effect on me. Or perhaps it was Deirdre and 'Dear Anne'.

I didn't fancy going into Burgerama with the gang in tow, so as soon as school was over I tried to slip off. Deirdre had gone into town with her mother on another leather jacket search but Therese caught up with me as I hurried down the school's main stairs.

'Ruth wants to go to the Health Food shop. She says the stuff in the school shop is full of sugar and salt and colourings. Want to come?' As she spoke Ruth emerged from a classroom munching a large packet of crisps. We looked at her accusingly.

'Well, I'm starving and this is all I can find till I get the healthy stuff,' she said guiltily, shoving the packet into her pocket.

'Yeah, but you were just going on about how bad that rubbish is for us,' Therese told her severely.

'Look, I've got to fly,' I said. 'Get something healthy for me.' And I dashed off leaving them looking after me suspiciously.

*　　*　　*

Some of my new-found confidence had oozed away by the time I arrived at Burgerama, but I forced myself to march in the way Therese always does.

There was no-one inside except Kev standing behind the gleaming counter wearing his striped apron and gulping down a can of Pepsi. Behind him burgers were sizzling on the grill.

I wasn't sure at first if he was pleased to see me. But

when our eyes met in The Look, I had the same stirred-up feeling as before.

We sat at a plastic-topped table which Kev cleared with expert speed. He even wiped it down with a J-cloth. I wondered if he did that at home. Philip wouldn't know what a J-cloth was.

Kev brought over two burgers on paper plates and a huge carton of chips. There are certainly advantages to having a boyfriend who works in a burger place. I was relieved that we were sitting well away from the window so no-one passing by could see us. I kept thinking the others might suspect something was up and follow me down here.

'What's the story with your brother?' Kev asked after a few moments.

My resentment that he hadn't bothered asking earlier melted away under his spell. Between mouthfuls I recounted the whole story. I finished, 'Mum and Dad went with Philip to the Garda Station. He had to make a statement admitting what he did and they all had to sign it.'

'What happens next?' asked Kev, dipping a chip into a pool of ketchup.

'They told Mum and Dad that 'cos it was a first offence Philip might not be charged but we'd have a visit from someone called a Juvenile Liaison Officer,' I explained. 'Dad says that means Philip'll get a warning but hopefully he won't have to go to court. At least it wouldn't be on his record.'

We went on eating. 'Philip's gone very quiet. He hasn't been near Sean,' I said. 'And yesterday, he actually went up to do his homework without anyone nagging him.'

'Ah, he'll be all right,' said Kev. 'Might make him get his act together.'

The door opened and two women laden with bags, buggies and noisy children came in and sat down at the next table. Kev stood up.

'I'd better go,' I said.

'Hang on, wait till I serve these.'

I sat quietly at the table watching him as he dished out an incredible number of burgers, cartons of chips and Cokes to the squealing children.

The two mothers somehow managed to talk cheerfully to each other and sip their coffees while feeding the kids, answering their questions and cleaning up the spills. I often wonder if you get special skills when you have kids. I hope so.

One of the women looked over at us as Kev came to sit beside me. She said something to her friend and they both turned and gave us encouraging smiles. I thought how great it was to be sitting in a cafe with a real boyfriend of my own just like in the stories in *Teen Dreams*.

I asked, 'How's Bernie?'

'Okay. She was asking if you'd like to come out to our place sometime. She'll give you a shout.' I nodded. But I couldn't help wondering how often Sinead had been to his house.

I jumped up and slung my bag over my shoulder. One of the kids was crawling towards us clutching a fistful of chips. He had tomato ketchup all over his face and was gurgling happily to himself. Another two were sitting on the floor under one of the tables playing with Coke cans and straws. The mothers were chatting unconcernedly, their table littered with half-eaten plates of food which they were finishing off as they talked.

At the door my heart lurched as Kev bent down and kissed me quite firmly and confidently. For a few dizzy seconds I forgot everything, even the women and the kids, and I was only aware of his mouth on mine and his body so close to me.

* * *

Outside I took a deep breath. It was a cool spring day, but I felt hot all over. I took off my sweater and draped it over my shoulders as I walked past the army barracks and crossed the road to the bus stop.

All I could think about was the kiss. We were actually getting better at kissing. But it raised all sorts of sensations which were new to me and which I'd only read about before.

I heard a shriek. Therese and Ruth had spotted me. They appeared at the bus stop beside me. Ruth was carrying a plastic bag from the Health Food shop. Therese had her mouth open ready to ask me where I'd been, so I said quickly to Ruth, 'What did you get?'

'I got a vitamin supplement, it says in the leaflet it's especially suitable for young adults – that's us – and brown rice for my mum,' she answered enthusiastically. 'D'you want a muesli bar? They're dried fruit and nuts, no sugar.'

Guiltily remembering the burger and chips I'd just demolished I shook my head. But at least I'd headed off a cross-examination.

On the bus they carefully avoided mentioning brothers, cars or guards. Instead we discussed the school fancy dress disco which was coming up soon after the exams.

But although I appeared to be taking an interest in the conversation, I was actually picturing myself at the disco looking irresistible with Kev beside me, probably in his dark blue sweatshirt because I just couldn't see him dressing up.

It would be the first time I'd ever gone to a disco with a boyfriend of my own. Then everyone would know it was definitely love.

The Interview

The next few days were tense in our house. We were all dreading the visit of the Juvenile Liaison Officer, who was coming to talk to Philip and Mum and Dad.

My mother rushed about looking anxious. Dad hurried in late for dinner every night. He was really trying to talk to Philip. They had boring conversations about football. Mum and I made an effort to join in but it wasn't easy. At least since the World Cup we knew what a penalty was.

Bernie rang on Saturday morning. I could hear Mum chatting to her when she answered the phone. There was much less hassle these days about my being friends with Bernie and Kev or about Ballytymon.

I knew Mum and Dad thought, like Nana, that Philip's friend Sean was a good bit to blame for the trouble they'd got into. So I suppose that's why they're more concerned now about what our friends are like rather than where they live. There's no more mention of 'right types'.

When I got to the phone Bernie said, 'Jackie, can you

come over on Wednesday? D'you get off early?' I could hear roars in the background and then loud banging. 'Sorry,' said Bernie. 'The kids are supposed to be in the video shop but they keep banging on the door of the phone box. There's a massive row about what video to get.'

Above the noise a child's voice wailed, 'You said we could get the *Ninja Turtles*.'

I said, 'Bernie, Wednesday's grand.'

There were more roars from the other end. Bernie let out a shout, 'Shut up all of you.' There was a sudden quiet.

'Sorry, Jackie.' Bernie's voice was gentle as usual again. She told me what bus to get and added, 'Kev'll meet you.' I liked the idea of that.

'See ya,' she said as she hung up.

I thought how hard it must be to come home from school and have to mind the kids. I was always knackered when I got home. I hoped Kev had told her about Philip and The Crime. I was sure she'd have something reassuring to say about it all.

*   *   *

I'd thought the tension at home was because of The Crime, but earlier in the week I'd heard Mum and Dad arguing in the kitchen. Like the previous row it seemed to be about money, and Mum had sounded really upset.

On Sunday when Nana and Gran came no-one talked much. Dad wore his worried frown. Philip was on his best behaviour. Gran kept repeating how delicious the food was, though it was the same roast chicken we always had. The subject of The Crime was avoided. And Nana didn't even mention my hair.

Nana went into the kitchen with Mum after lunch and they were in there for ages. Afterwards she seemed very quiet and I noticed Mum's eyes were red. She said she had a cold but it didn't sound very convincing.

All this made me wonder if it was The Crime alone that everyone was so wound up about, or was it also this money problem. It was difficult to ask, and it was clear they didn't want to say.

* * *

When the interview finally came it was a relief. Dad actually came home early for it.

Instead of a uniformed guard, I was surprised to see a young woman in a red jacket and short skirt carrying a briefcase. She smiled as she shook hands with all of us.

'I'm the Juvenile Liaison Officer, JLO for short,' she said brightly. 'I've just come to have a chat with Philip and his parents.'

They all looked quite cheerful, even Philip, as they went into the study. The door closed firmly behind them.

I went upstairs to do my homework, which was taking longer and longer as summer exams approached. All the teachers were giving us lectures about revision and talking about 'buckling down to work'. Miss Kinsella had even said we shouldn't be watching any TV except the news. There was an incredulous gasp from the class when she added, 'Not even "Neighbours" or "Home and Away".'

After about half an hour I heard the study door open and the sound of polite farewells in the hall. With relief I stopped wrestling with my maths and ran downstairs.

Mum was actually smiling as she shut the front door behind the JLO.

'Well?' I asked.

'It wasn't too bad,' Mum said. 'She was very nice.'

'Is she really a guard?' I asked. 'She doesn't look like one.'

'Yes, she told us some of the guards who're interested in social work volunteer for this Juvenile Liaison scheme.'

Dad turned to Philip. He asked him quietly, 'Are you sure you understood everything she said?'

Philip nodded, trying to look serious.

'What did she say?' I demanded. I felt I should have been included in the interview, seeing that I'd had to deal with Philip, Nana, the guards and all the hassle.

'She had a file on Philip and Sean and asked lots of questions about the family, and whether any of us had any drink or drugs problems,' said my mother. 'Thank goodness we haven't.'

'Actually I could do with a gin and tonic,' said Dad. We looked at him. Unusually for him these days, he was grinning instead of frowning. I thought how long it was since he'd made a joke, even a feeble one.

Philip was getting chirpy now the ordeal was over. 'I'm starving,' he said, rushing into the kitchen.

I suddenly felt hungry myself, even though I'd had a Twix bar on the way home. It must be the stress again. I followed Philip into the kitchen.

'What did the JLO say to you?' I asked him.

He thought for a bit. 'Dunno,' he said finally.

I said to Mum, 'Well, Philip seems to be back to his usual self.'

*   *   *

After tea, when Philip had gone to watch TV, Dad told me more.

'She wanted Philip to tell her exactly what he'd done. Then she asked if he knew it was wrong, and why. He told her he would never do anything like it again.' Mum poured the tea.

'Will he have to go to court?' I asked.

'Apparently if it's a first offence for both lads they take into account their age and family background. She said they probably won't be charged, but Philip will have to go to the Garda Station and the Superintendent will give him a warning about his behaviour, what did she call it, Eithne?'

'A formal caution,' Mum replied.

Dad went to empty the rubbish into the bin outside the back door. Philip, assuming the coast was clear, appeared back in the kitchen to see if there was any more food. But Dad came back in just as Philip was in the act of sneaking a handful of biscuits from the tin. He raised his voice. 'So as I was saying, he won't have to go to court as long as he's very careful in the future.'

He glared at Philip who was about to creep back to the TV, and went on deliberately, 'The JLO said they have about an 85 percent success rate, that means the guards never hear about them again. And Philip had better be one of the 85 percent.'

'He's very lucky,' Mum added. 'I just hope he's learned his lesson.' Everyone looked at Philip.

He mumbled with his mouth full what sounded like 'lots of homework' as he retreated out of the kitchen.

Mum sighed as he went out, 'I just hope we never have to go through anything like this again,' she said. 'It's taken years off us.'

I went into the living-room to watch 'Home and Away'. After a few minutes Philip came in, still chewing.

It was blissfully quiet, thanks to our temporary truce. Soaps have their plus side.

* * *

'Well,' asked Deirdre, 'How'd it go?'

She'd called round on her bike the next evening to hear the latest in the Philip saga, but I suspected it was the Kev saga that really interested her.

She came up to my room and I put on my new Kate Bush album and moved a heap of clothes from the chair so that she could sit down. She was wearing jeans and a denim shirt that she'd borrowed from Therese, and her soft dark hair was caught up in a ponytail. I noticed that I didn't feel the usual stab of envy at how pretty she looked. It must be my new-found confidence. I just hoped it would last.

'First things first,' I began. 'Any luck with the leather jacket?'

'Well, I covered the Ilac Centre, Mary Street and Henry Street. I even went to Clery's with my mum.' She chewed on a strand of hair, a habit we're all trying to get her out of at her own request.

She went on, 'There were only two possibles, but they both cost a bomb, even though I only have to pay half.'

We both jumped as the front door slammed. It sounded as though an army was marching up the stairs. I opened my door. 'It's all right, it's only Philip coming home from football practice,' I told her.

'Whatever happened about Philip?' she asked, as the door of his room banged and Heavy Metal music blared, almost drowning out 'The Red Shoes'.

I told her about the JLO's visit. 'Mum says he's lucky, if it wasn't for this scheme he'd have to appear in the Children's Court. Dad's really pissed off 'cos he's had to pay for the damage to the neighbours' cars.'

I thought about mentioning Dad's money troubles to Deirdre, but there was nothing concrete to tell her really, just remarks and incidents that made me feel things weren't right.

We listened to Kate Bush, and I dashed off a portrait of the JLO in her red suit to add to the portrait gallery in the back of my French book.

Deirdre glanced down at it. 'She's cool.' She caught sight of the portrait of Kev with The Look. 'What about him?' she asked. 'Any developments?'

I brought her up to date on how things stood with Kev, about the two kisses, about my improved confidence, but also how frustrating it was when he didn't make contact.

And always in the back of my mind was The Scene. Sinead's portrait was there in *Français Aujourd'hui* so I couldn't forget her even if I tried.

'Going to his house may be a good idea,' Deirdre said when I'd finished. She was trying out my frosted pink nail varnish on her long beautiful nails. I looked at my short stubby ones, chewed round the edges in times of stress, which were rather frequent these days.

She went on, 'It could give you an insight into his personal family relationships and help him to relate to you as a girlfriend.'

'Yeah,' I agreed doubtfully.

Then Deirdre said carelessly, 'I saw Andy the other day.'

I stared at her. 'I thought you were back with Mark.'

'Yeah, well, Andy called round and went on and on about himself, I couldn't get a word in. Mum kept hovering about to get a look at him.'

'What did he want?' I asked. 'Apart from going on about himself?'

'Well, eventually he asked me to meet him in Pizza Paradise. I said I wasn't sure.'

'Are you going to?'

'I might. I'm getting fed up with Mark, he's so serious. And I don't like kissing him much. It's not a bit like you said you felt with Kev.'

She finished her nails and spread out her hands. We both looked at them admiringly. I resolved there and then to stop chewing my nails, stress or no stress.

She waggled her fingers and put on a faraway look. 'I just thought kissing Andy might be nicer, even though he's so full of himself.'

I knew what she meant about Andy. He was really hunky.

I said wickedly, 'Surely a long-standing relationship with a solid reliable lad like Mark shouldn't be thrown away just because a good-looking hunk snaps his fingers at you?' I'd like to write those columns myself, it's all so easy when it's about someone else.

Deirdre grabbed my cuddly animals from the bed and pelted me with them. After a bit we called a truce and put on Sinead O'Connor.

Next door Philip turned up the volume on Metallica. I heard a faint cry from downstairs.

I said to Deirdre, 'Mum just said, turn down the noise, the house is shaking.'

'How can you tell?' she asked wonderingly.

'Long experience.'

'How's Philip behaving these days? Did that guard come yet?' Nana, her hair stiffly waved and curled by Marcel, was pouring out two cups of tea for us in her tidy kitchen. She was making sandwiches for her bridge night. I'd called round with a cream sponge baked by my mother.

I said, 'He's more or less back to normal.' She looked disapproving.

I added, 'I don't think he'll do anything like that again. Sean doesn't come round anymore.'

I told her about Philip's interview with the JLO. 'Hopefully he'll get this warning from the Superintendent, and he won't have to go to court,' I explained, nibbling the trimmings from the sandwiches.

'Well, that's a relief,' said Nana, sipping her tea. 'I just hope not too many people hear about it. I didn't even tell my bridge partners.'

'Nana, does it matter so much about people knowing?' I couldn't help asking. 'Dad says what really matters is that Philip should realise he's done something wrong and dangerous.'

'Of course that's important,' said Nana, 'I've often warned them about Philip getting into bad company.' She added firmly, 'But you don't want the world to know your business.'

It seemed to be time to change the subject. Taking an iced fairy cake I asked, 'How's Auntie Gemma?'

'All right,' said Nana briefly. 'I'm going down to stay with her soon.' Like Mum, Nana didn't think I should know about such things as hysterectomies, so I had to pretend I didn't know what kind of operation it was. Nana was under the impression that we didn't learn about the womb in biology.

I never liked to tell her we'd started sex education ages ago. Not that it had been much help, I reflected, when it came to kissing Kev.

I left Nana folding little flowery paper serviettes. As I was going out the door she appeared with a bag of fairy cakes.

'Mind you share them with Philip,' she said as she kissed me goodbye. 'He may be bold, but he still needs feeding.'

The Visit

On the rare occasions I went to Ballytymon, usually to the shopping centre, I was always surprised by the brilliant view of the Dublin mountains from the bus.

The sky was grey and it looked like rain, but there were daffodils in bloom along the Ballytymon bypass.

Getting away had been easier than I'd expected. Mum was rushing out to watch Philip play in a school football match, and when I said I was going to Bernie's she just nodded and said, 'Don't be late back. I've got my Yoga class tonight and Dad'll be late home, so I want you to keep an eye on Philip.'

I'd spent ages getting ready, putting on clothes and throwing them off after one look in the mirror. I finally settled on baggy stonewashed jeans which belonged to Deirdre, a black U2 T-shirt, and my denim jacket. The ankle boots were a bit scuffed but they'd have to do.

Kev was waiting at the stop when the bus arrived at Ballytymon village. Although he only said 'Hi,' and brushed my cheek with his lips, my heart lifted.

I wonder why I never feel like this with anyone else. Deirdre says that's one of the signs of true love. Maybe she's right and it's just my negative attitude which makes me have doubts.

On the way to Kev's house I told him the latest about Philip. 'Mum and Dad are trying to give him more attention,' I said. 'It's getting a bit sickening. Mum's just gone to see him play football, and I know she hates watching games.'

We passed a modern-looking school, all glass and brick, with green lawns and trees around it. 'My sisters go there,' said Kev as we turned into an estate of small neat houses.

There were crowds of kids playing in the road and dashing in and out of open front doors. Mothers holding babies were chatting in front gardens or pushing buggies laden with kids and shopping. We walked along holding hands. It came quite naturally now.

I was feeling nervous at the thought of meeting Kev's sisters and his mother. I tried to summon up the new confidence. At least I know Bernie, I told myself, and she'll be pleased to see me.

At Kev's house a small brown dog was curled up in the porch. It came bounding over and jumped up eagerly to lick us. Two little girls were playing with a Barbie doll in the garden and they hurried over too. One had long fair hair like Bernie's. She tugged at Kev's jeans, and he scooped her up in a practised sort of way.

'Is that her?' she whispered to him.

'Yeah, this is Jackie,' he said grinning. 'Jackie, meet Sharon and Fiona.'

The dog jumped up on them, yapping excitedly. 'And this is Dustin,' Kev added.

The kids seemed much quieter than they'd sounded when Bernie had phoned me. Maybe that had just been a bad day.

I'd rarely seen Kev so relaxed and cheerful. It was strange to think he was part of a family. I'd really only thought of him in relation to me and my feelings. For once Deirdre's advice, or rather Dear Anne's, was right on.

Inside the warm bright kitchen there was lots of activity. An older girl was doing homework at the table, the radio was blaring, toys and schoolbooks were spread around and the kettle was boiling furiously.

In the middle of all this Bernie was making sandwiches, looking as tranquil as ever. She hugged me and took my jacket.

Soon we were all squashed round the table eating huge platefuls of sandwiches and fruit cake and drinking tea and fizzy orange.

'Lisa's having trouble with her homework,' Bernie said to me. 'Are you any good at Irish?'

'Not great.' The girls all looked at me and giggled.

I carried on eating with the kids staring as I took each mouthful. I was beginning to feel as if I had two heads. Even the dog was looking at me with liquid brown eyes.

Bernie said, sharply for her, 'Stop staring, you kids. Where's your manners?' At this they dropped their eyes and started to giggle again.

Bernie turned to me and shrugged apologetically. 'Sorry Jackie. Don't mind them.'

Lisa lifted the wriggling dog on to her lap and fed it bits of cheese sandwich at which it became ecstatic.

'Hey Lisa, don't give Dustin our tea,' said Kev, reaching for another sandwich.

Bernie looked at me with a sigh. 'They're desperate sometimes.'

I asked her, 'What happened that day you phoned me, when they were arguing over which video to get?'

She shook her head warningly. 'Don't remind them about the *Ninja Turtles*, or there'll be war.'

Kev jumped up as we heard a key in the lock. The front door closed and a small thin woman came in carrying several Quinnsworth bags.

The dog dashed over to her and jumped up and down yapping and licking. She reached down and patted him. She had greying dark hair and her face was sad. You could see she had once been pretty.

Kev went over and took the bags from her while Bernie poured her a cup of tea. My mother never got that sort of attention from Philip or me.

She smiled at me and said gently, 'I'm glad you could come, Jackie, I've heard all about you.' I wondered what she'd heard and whether it was from Bernie or Kev.

I smiled, but I couldn't get a word in because the girls all started to talk to her at once.

'Comin' to the match, Ma?' asked Lisa.

At this stage they'd all stopped staring at me, except Dustin. He'd come back to me and was sitting on my foot looking up soulfully. Seeing no-one was looking I gave him a bit of fruit cake.

'You're never still into girls' football?' teased Kev, sitting down and reaching for another piece of cake. 'Packie Bonner better watch out.'

'Ooh-Ah, Paul McGrath,' squealed Fiona, and they all exploded into giggles. Dustin barked in sympathy.

Bernie turned to me. 'They're all into football since the World Cup,' she said. 'We're all going up to the park to watch Lisa in goal.'

'She can't even catch, she'll make a show of us,' said the youngest girl, Sharon scathingly, tossing her long fair hair. And she'd looked so angelic.

Lisa turned on her furiously. This was getting like tea at home with Philip.

Bernie let out a shout. 'Shut up all of you. Let Ma have her tea in peace. What'll Jackie think?'

Their mother, who had eaten nothing but just sipped at her tea, rose and said wearily, 'I'm just going upstairs to lie down. I'll come up to the park later. Try and keep them quiet Bernie, poor Jackie's probably getting a headache.' She had a little crease in her forehead and looked as though she was the one who had the headache.

I said, 'I've got a young brother, he can make more noise than all of these put together.'

* * *

After we'd cleared away the tea things, Kev disappeared upstairs. The three girls ran squealing into the garden with the dog beside itself with excitement, yapping and jumping at their heels.

Bernie asked me what had happened about Philip. Kev had apparently mentioned The Crime, but true to form, hadn't told her much.

She listened sympathetically as I related the story.

'The JLO wasn't as bad as we'd thought,' I finished. 'But Mum and Dad are still pretty shook up by it all.'

'Well, maybe it's no harm if your brother got a fright. It's easy to get into bad company, my ma's always worrying about us.'

'I sometimes wonder why people have kids if all they do is worry about them,' I said half to myself.

We gazed out of the window into the garden where Fiona and Sharon were kicking a football, which was nearly as big as they were, towards a makeshift goal between two sweaters. Lisa, aided by the dog, was flinging herself at the ball in a desperate attempt to make a save.

Bernie swished some water round the sink. 'I s'pose there wouldn't be much crack without them,' she said. 'It's worth the hassle.'

Between the squeals from the garden I suddenly heard

the distant sound of a guitar. I looked at Bernie.

She said, 'Go on up to Kev's room, I'll give you a shout when we're going to the match.' Hesitantly I climbed the stairs and followed the music.

The walls of Kev's room were covered with posters of U2 and The Fat Lady Sings. He was sitting on the bed strumming the guitar. He had the serious look, and his hair flopped into his eyes the way I liked.

I sat on the floor listening. He didn't move, we didn't kiss, but I felt a surge of warmth and happiness just from being with him.

Surely he must feel the same, I thought, even though neither of us said anything.

*   *   *

Later we all went to the park to watch the football.

Kev was wearing the denim jacket he always wore when we used to exchange The Look at the bus stop. Lisa was decked out in World Cup football gear. She rushed off to where the two all-girl teams were gathered beside the pitch.

Even though the sky had darkened and rain was falling there were lots of families with kids and babies in buggies watching from the sidelines.

As soon as the match began there was great shouting and roaring from the spectators. Two track-suited women coaches darted up and down shouting encouragement, and the referee, the only man on the pitch, had to keep blowing his whistle to be heard above the roars.

When Lisa saved a goal just before half-time everyone nearly went berserk, the little girls shrieking and jumping up and down, Kev waving his hands in the air and chanting, 'Olé, Olé, Olé, Olé.' Even their mother clapped, a slight flush in her pale cheeks. She caught my eye and smiled her sad, sweet smile before being pulled away by the girls to where Lisa's team were huddled on the grass chattering excitedly and mopping the sweat from their faces.

During half-time a couple of lads came over to where I stood with Kev and Bernie. One of them said, 'Hiya, Jackie.' It was Andy. He looked cool, even in a sweatshirt with the hood up.

Before I could reply he said abruptly, 'What's the story with Deirdre? She said she'd meet me and then she didn't show. She's not back with that moron, is she?'

'Mark's okay,' I said defensively. After all, a computer expert, even a boring one, could hardly be a moron.

'Anyway,' I went on, 'she didn't hear from you for ages. You can't expect her to be available whenever you show up.' Therese would be pleased with that, I thought.

Andy frowned. It was clear he wasn't used to criticism.

I knew Deirdre was torn between Andy and Mark but I agreed with Therese that Andy wasn't really serious. But then Therese had a pretty poor opinion of most fellas and their intentions.

After a bit Andy said casually, 'How're things with you

and Kev?' He shook off his hood so that I could admire his profile.

'Okay,' I said shortly, changing the subject before Kev could overhear. 'You still working in Dunnes?' I asked him.

'Yeah, the few quid's useful,' he said. 'I had a go at the checkout, it was a panic.' You could see him turning on the charm. 'There was this oul' wan with about twenty tins of cat food. Just for the crack I asked her if she was opening a Chinese takeaway. The fella behind her hit the roof, turns out he works in the Chinese takeaway in the village. Said he'd report me.'

I couldn't help laughing. 'Did he?' I asked.

'Nah, I said I didn't mean it. It was only a bit of crack. I don't make any more jokes at the checkout though.'

* * *

The whistle blew and everyone turned their attention to the match again.

I looked round the park while the game continued and noticed a figure on the other side of the pitch who seemed to be staring in our direction. It was hard to tell in the now persistent drizzle whether it was a girl or a guy. I could just make out white trousers and a dark jacket.

I was about to point out the figure to Bernie who was standing near me with one of her sisters hanging on to her. But when I looked again whoever it was had vanished.

Kev, who'd been kicking a ball around with some of the lads, came over and stood beside me. I thought, if we were on our own he'd put his arm round me. The thought made me shiver.

Reluctantly I said to him, 'I'd better get going. I told Mum I wouldn't be late, I've got to mind Philip.'

'I'll walk you to the bus,' he said.

Bernie gave me a hug. 'Come over again,' she said smiling. She turned back to the match, holding Sharon by the hand. Their mother was talking to a neighbour and waved and smiled as we walked off.

When we'd gone some distance Kev put his arm round me. I felt great, the visit had gone okay and we seemed to be getting closer all the time.

The bus stop was deserted. Kev waited with me till the bus came. We didn't talk much, just stood very close together.

After a while I said, 'Your mum's brilliant.'

His face took on a tense look. 'She's been better the last few days.' He added fiercely, 'If the oul' fella'd just leave her alone she'd be grand.'

I squeezed his hand. 'Don't mind him,' I whispered.

'You sound like Bernie,' he said, giving one of his rare smiles. I looked straight into his grey eyes and felt almost breathless. But before we had a chance to kiss the bus roared up.

I jumped on and climbed the stairs. Looking down I saw Kev walking away from the bus stop. I sat in a warm glow thinking about him and his family and whether I was going to fit in with them.

The bus lurched off and a girl brushed past my seat and sat down directly in front of me. I was enveloped in a cloud of perfume. She had spiky red hair and wore white jeans and a shiny black bomber jacket.

A faint sense of danger stirred inside me as I sat staring at her back. Then I remembered the figure I'd seen in the distance at the match. As the bus gathered speed the girl suddenly turned and glared at me.

It was Sinead, the ex-girlfriend, and my heart sank as I realised that this time I was on my own.

The Punch

I sat motionless, feeling as if I'd been punched in the stomach. I hadn't forgotten Sinead but she'd got pushed to the back of my mind.

After all I'd had a lot to think about, what with everything that had happened at home, and the visit to Kev's house, and now the exams looming.

Sinead looked at me contemptuously through half-closed eyes. 'You think you've got your claws into him, don't you?' she said, a taunting smile on her perfectly made-up face.

Shook up though I was I couldn't help wondering how her eyes didn't close from the sheer weight of all the stuff on them. And there was a tidemark round her chin where her make-up ended.

I knew I had to keep my nerve. I thought of Therese and tried to summon up some assertiveness. Swallowing hard I said, 'Whatever's between Kev and me is none of your business.' My voice came out sounding squeaky, but

I was proud of myself all the same.

Sinead ran her fingers with their long purple-painted nails through her spiky hair. I wondered why none of them were chipped or broken, let alone chewed like mine. Maybe they were false.

'Listen, you leave him alone,' she said. 'I'm pissed off with you messing around with him. He only goes out with you 'cos his stupid cow of a sister keeps pushing him.'

My heart started to thump. It was true Bernie was my friend and she'd helped things along between Kev and me, but I hadn't imagined her pushing Kev to go out with me.

A flicker of doubt stirred in my mind, but I said as firmly as I could, 'It's got nothing to do with Bernie.'

'Oh yeah, so why did she give him stink for going out with me last Saturday?' I was stunned, though I tried not to show it. I thought back to Saturday. I'd babysat for the Nolans and started some biology revision. Kev had said he had to work late at Burgerama and would try and give me a shout on Sunday. After that I hadn't heard anything until today's visit to Ballytymon.

My mind raced. Surely he wasn't going out with the two of us at the same time?

My shock must have shown, because Sinead's tone softened. She must have thought she'd won. She fluttered her mascara'd eyelashes.

'Look, I've been going with Kev for years. He just doesn't know his own mind sometimes. I know he really wants me. You find someone of your own sort.'

I felt a wave of anger. 'What d'you mean, my own sort? You sound like my dad. Bernie and Kev are my sort, we get on great, he's the first guy I've ever –'

I stopped. All the doubts came flooding back. To my horror, tears came to my eyes. I blinked and stared hard out of the window. The last thing I wanted was to make a show of myself in front of Sinead.

Fortunately the familiar streets of Rathnure came into view. In my haste to get away I got off two stops early.

As the bus drove off I saw her sharp profile, a heavy silver earring dangling. She turned and gave a mocking wave.

* * *

I was glad of the walk home, even in the driving rain.

My mind seethed. I remembered Andy's remark in Pizza Paradise about Sinead thinking she was a film star. I had to admit she'd given a great performance.

Is Kev playing us off against each other? I asked myself. If so, why does he make me feel I'm the only girl he wants? And what am I to do now? Should I be the one to break it up?

As I turned into our road the unanswered questions piled up in my mind.

Why had Bernie said nothing when I was there today about Kev going out with Sinead? Maybe it wasn't true. Why, since I'd met Kev, had my life become so complicated?

Whatever did I think about before all this?

And even if it was really love, I wondered, was it worth it?

The Message

'**M**um, will you sponsor me?' Philip spoke through a mouthful of Rice Krispies, cramming toast and marmalade into his mouth with his free hand.

'Morning Ireland' blared away on the radio but no-one was listening. Mum, in her yellow flowery dressing-gown, was making the tea.

'Don't talk with your mouth full, Philip,' she said automatically as she filled the teapot. 'Sponsor you for what?'

'Dunno. I think it's wheelchairs or something.' Philip slurped up another spoonful of cereal and took a huge bite of toast.

Dad lowered the *Irish Times*. You could see he was trying to take an interest in Philip's activities, while ignoring his table manners. 'If it's the Wheelchair Association it's a very good cause,' he said. 'What've you got to do, is it walking or swimming or what?'

Philip gulped down half a cup of tea. When he'd finished he had a brown moustache.

'Knitting,' he mumbled.

We all looked up. 'AA Road Watch' babbled away on the radio. There seemed to be roadworks everywhere. Dad usually gave out about it, but all attention was on Philip.

'Knitting?' asked Dad , incredulous. 'Surely you've got it wrong?' Mum sat down with a cup of tea and a bowl of muesli and bran. I knew I should have had that instead of toast and coffee. Ruth was always going on about the importance of fibre, but Deirdre said that bran tasted like grated cardboard, and it does, a bit.

Philip mumbled, 'Well, we had to tell the teacher if we're doing swimming or knitting and I'm not allowed do swimming 'cos Sean and me splashed the mothers –'

'Splashed? You mean drenched,' I said, remembering the row at the time when Mum had been called to see an angry PE teacher.

'– so I've got to do the knitting,' Philip finished, producing a crumpled sponsorship card.

Mum said, trying not to laugh, 'But you can't knit.'

Philip looked hurt. 'I can so, Gran showed me. Anyway, Jackie can do it.'

I glared at him. I was feeling really fed up that morning. The exams were coming up fast. And my love life, which had seemed so promising, was now zilch.

I'd more or less decided that if Kev really did go out with Sinead last Saturday, then I'd have to break it off with him. But how was I to find out the truth? Life these days seemed to be one big problem.

So instead of ignoring Philip's nonsense I turned on him. 'You're such a pathetic little chauvinist. Why should I knit for you? Just piss off and leave me alone.' I jumped up and went to get an apple and banana for break, something else we were all nagged into by Ruth.

My mother looked at me reproachfully. In the morning light her face looked pale and tired, and even her highlights seemed to have gone dull.

Dad put down his cup and the *Irish Times* with a sigh. As he left the kitchen he said to Mum, 'Eithne, I'll be late tonight, I'll grab a sandwich at the office.'

Mum followed him into the hall. She said something to him in a low voice. I couldn't hear properly over the noise of the radio and Philip's loud slurping, but I thought Dad mentioned something about 'working on the discrepancies'.

I wondered what sort of discrepancies he meant.

'Morning Ireland' had gone on to the 'Sports Round-up'. Mum came back into the kitchen looking wearier than ever. She shook her head. 'He'll get an ulcer, he had really bad indigestion last night.'

Philip was still munching. He said plaintively, 'Look, Dad's gone off and he didn't sign my sponsor card.'

'Really, Philip, you're so selfish,' I told him. 'Ask Nana and Gran to sponsor you.' I added nastily. 'You could go with Nana to Marcel and knit together under the drier.'

As I dashed into the hall to get my coat he aimed a punch at me and upset Dad's unfinished cup of tea all over the *Irish Times*. From the hall I could see poor old Mum mopping the kitchen table with a long-suffering look.

I felt guilty. Dad had told me we were supposed to be patient with Philip and encourage his interests. I supposed that included unexpected ones like knitting. He hadn't been to see the Garda Superintendent yet to get a caution and I knew Mum was still worried about it all.

I picked up my bag which weighed a ton with all the revision books and put my head round the kitchen door.

'All right, I'll sponsor you as long as I don't have to wear anything you've knitted.' I was rewarded with a smile from Mum and a grunt from Philip.

I shut the front door and ran for the bus.

* * *

School was dreary, with everyone giving out about work, exams and revision.

'Fifth year is not to be regarded as a dossing year,' said Miss Kinsella in English class. 'I hope you all understand that.'

There was an unenthusiastic mumble from the class. Ruth whispered, 'Honestly, they don't give you a chance to doss even if you wanted to.'

Miss Kinsella went on, 'These exams are part of your preparation for the Leaving Cert, and your future career depends on that.' She looked severely round the class at people slumped dejectedly over their desks. Everyone avoided catching her eye.

I looked over at Deirdre. She was chewing a strand of

hair and staring into the distance. Was she thinking about Mark or Andy? I suspected it was Andy.

As Miss Kinsella went on about careers I tried to imagine what mine might be. Maybe with all my recent experience of relationships and their problems I could be a social worker or perhaps an agony aunt along with Deirdre. I could see us confidently drinking coffee in a luxurious office while a queue of anxious people waited for our advice.

I came to with a start when the bell rang for break.

In the canteen I noticed that all our gang had brought an identical healthy lunch, a tribute to Ruth's influence. All round us people munched crisps and chocolate biscuits and swigged Diet Cokes and Pepsis.

'I just hope this is doing us some good,' said Deirdre gloomily peeling her banana. 'I could do with a Yorkie.'

'Exams piss me off,' moaned Therese. 'It's just not fair, everything depending on a few hours in one day.'

'Yeah, and s'pose you're feeling in bad form that day or you've got the flu,' said Ruth eagerly. 'That often happens to me in exams.'

We all exchanged glances, which weren't lost on Ruth.

She said heatedly, 'Well, surely you've sometimes had the flu or something when you're doing exams?'

'Yeah, but for you, Ruth, having the flu or something is a way of life,' Deirdre said unkindly.

I could see Ruth was offended and that would probably bring on a headache, so I put in quickly, 'Anyone had any

bright ideas about what to wear for the fancy dress disco?'
I felt a stab as I mentioned it because I'd planned to bring
Kev. Now everything involving Kev was uncertain.

The bell rang for class, and we set off in various
directions humping our bagfuls of books, resigned to the
depressing prospect of more revision and pep-talks.

At least there wasn't time for even more depressing
thoughts about Kev and me and our future, if we had one.

*   *   *

Later that evening I was sitting in my room reading *Biology
for Today*. I was trying to memorise a cross-section of the
earthworm.

The scent of newly cut grass wafted up from the garden
through the open window.

I heard the distant sound of the doorbell and in spite of
my resolution to concentrate on revision, I felt my heart
jump in that familiar way as Mum called up, 'Jackie, some
of your friends are here.' She sounded disapproving.

I rushed downstairs, full of irrational hope. Could Kev
have come to explain everything and reassure me that it
was love after all, just like might happen in *Teen Dreams?*

Instead, Deirdre and Therese were standing at the door.

'Sorry for interrupting the revision, Jackie,' Deirdre said
loudly, for my mother's benefit. 'Can you come out for a
few minutes?'

She gave me a meaningful look, and Therese put her
hand on my shoulder and gently guided me down the front

path. Mum had gone into the kitchen, deliberately leaving the front door wide open.

To my surprise, I saw Andy lounging on the low garden wall. He was wearing a white shirt open nearly to the waist, so that we could all see the hair on his chest.

'Hi, Jackie,' he said, as we sat beside him on the wall in a row.

Although it wasn't Kev, my spirits lifted, just from being outside in the soft spring air with the crowd, instead of cooped up in my room with *Biology for Today* and the earthworm.

I had to admit Andy looked really good. You could see he knew it the way he smoothed back his longish curly hair and grinned easily.

He jerked his head at Mum's white Starlet, parked in the driveway. 'Nice little car,' he said patronisingly.

Therese said, 'Andy's got a message. I'm here to make sure he gets it right.'

Andy said mockingly, 'That's right, Therese, never trust a fella.'

Therese silenced him with one of the fierce looks she must have perfected at her assertiveness class. She clearly wasn't knocked out by Andy like everyone else.

'Get on with it,' she said sharply, giving him a nudge with her elbow.

He grinned at me. 'Well,' he drawled, 'Bernie said to tell you they'd all be up in the Ballytymon shopping centre tomorrow morning, and could you ever come and meet them in Bewley's.' He smoothed his hair again.

Therese threw him an irritated look. 'Tell her about Kev,' she hissed.

'Oh yeah, Kev said to say he'll be there.'

I looked from Andy to Therese suspiciously. 'Wait now, why couldn't Kev tell me himself?'

'He's at work, their mum's wrecked her ankle and the kids were sick. They've all been up to their eyes.'

'And Kev only heard yesterday about Sinead having a go at you on the bus,' Deirdre put in. 'I told Therese and she told Andy and he told Kev.'

Why was my love life, if you could call it that, the main topic of discussion for everyone? Still, at least now there was a chance to talk to Kev and Bernie and find out the truth.

Deirdre and Therese were looking at me uneasily. I knew I should be more grateful that I had friends who tried to help me sort out my life.

Andy jumped down from the wall. He smiled directly at Deirdre in that lazy way that really gets to you. I could almost feel her melting. 'I'll walk you home.'

Deirdre threw me an apologetic look as they went off. They walked quite close together but didn't touch. It looked as though things were on again between them. How would Mark feel about that? I wondered. At least he had his computer to console him. All I had were the Romantic poets and the earthworm.

'These lads really piss me off,' said Therese as we

watched them go. 'The sooner we forget them and do our own thing, the better.'

'Oh Therese,' I said, 'you're dead right. This love business is a pain. They don't tell you that in *Teen Dreams*.'

'Well, if you meet Kev tomorrow make sure he doesn't walk all over you,' said Therese. 'I'd better go home and look at *Hamlet*. If only he wasn't such a weed.'

Did she mean Hamlet or Kev? I was afraid to ask.

I crept past the kitchen where I could hear Mum clattering dishes, and went back up to the earthworm. Maybe he and I have something in common. After all, he gets walked on too.

The Last Straw

Mum and Dad weren't too pleased when I told them casually that I was popping out for an hour or two to meet the others for coffee. I was deliberately vague about the details.

Mum said sharply, 'You've got your exams next week,' as if she were announcing something I didn't know. 'What with going off for coffee and people calling round I don't see you doing much revision.'

'Don't get us wrong,' Dad said hastily. 'We don't mind any of your friends coming over normally.' I knew he was remembering the row we'd had about the Ballytymon crowd.

He went on, 'But these exams are important. The Leaving Cert will be coming up faster than you think, and if you want to go on to third level ...'

I groaned inwardly. Wherever I went these days I kept hearing about third level, careers, the future. I knew these things were important but it was very stressful.

Dad added, half to himself, 'That's if we can afford third level –'

I was so preoccupied by the approaching meeting with Bernie and Kev that I ignored this remark, and only thought of it again much later. I said as patiently as I could, 'Look, the Leaving's not till next year and I'll do my best when it comes. But it's not going to make much difference if I go out for a while this morning. Even Miss Kinsella thinks we should take a break sometimes.'

Well, I'm sure she does, even if she hasn't actually said so.

To my surprise, they seemed to accept that. Mum just added automatically, 'Don't be late for lunch.'

I remembered the 'Dear Anne' column suggesting we should have rational discussions with parents about problems rather than angry silences or shouting matches.

It certainly worked this time, better than rushing up to my room in floods of tears, slamming the door and throwing myself on the bed, which was what I used to do.

* * *

So I found myself at the Ballytymon shopping centre, decked out in black leggings and a long brown jacket that came down to my knees, that Mum and Dad detested but Deirdre liked.

The place was busy and I wandered round the shops, feeling sick with anticipation. Eventually I bumped into Deirdre and Therese going into a boutique. Deirdre had said they might be here this morning as it was one of the few places in Dublin that she hadn't yet sussed out for a leather jacket.

I went in with them and we all prowled around. After we'd looked at everything in the shop at least twice, we squeezed into the crowded dressing room. Deirdre took in a leather jacket and a black mini, and Therese had jeans and a shirt. I felt too stressed out to try on anything.

All round us girls were dressing and undressing rapidly. Everyone had a little heap of clothes at their feet and most people had at least one friend with them, either staring at them critically, or standing about looking bored.

Deirdre looked cool in the leather jacket, but she decided it was the wrong shade for her hair and it cost too much anyway, so she ended up with the mini-skirt. It occurred to me that Deirdre had acquired a lot of other clothes while on the trail of the leather jacket.

Therese complained that the jeans were too baggy, and the shirt too tight.

It got hotter and hotter and I couldn't wait to escape. I had the peculiar feeling in my stomach that I used to have whenever I saw Kev, and I hadn't even seen him yet.

Eventually everyone was dressed. We parted outside the boutique. Deirdre, under pressure from her mother, was going home to do revision, and Therese was heading off to aerobics.

Deirdre gave me a hug and a last piece of advice. 'Jackie, if you can't trust the guy it's better for both of you if you finish it.'

I knew it was true, but it didn't make me feel any better. She added, 'Sure you don't want us to stick around?'

'Thanks a million, but I've really got to deal with this myself.' I sounded more confident than I felt.

Therese fixed me with the assertive look. 'Remember, you're a woman not a mouse.' She'd said that before, and it hadn't been much help then either.

She went on firmly, 'Just because you like his sister, that's no reason to get messed around by him.'

I watched them go, my head spinning from all the advice and assertiveness. But I knew that in the end I'd be depending on Bernie to sort things out.

*　　*　　*

Although Bewley's was crowded I spotted them straight away. Bernie was wearing a black poloneck and jeans. Her glossy golden hair was tied back in a ponytail and she looked pale.

Her sisters were sitting round a table eating huge doughnuts. They had cream and jam smeared all over their faces. Their mother was bringing a cup of black coffee over to the table. She was limping and I could see her ankle was bandaged. So there was at least some truth in Andy's report.

Kev wasn't with them. I felt both relieved and disappointed.

The youngest girl, Sharon, must have recognised me because she nudged Bernie. They all rushed over and Lisa even gave me a hug. Above their heads Bernie's serious grey eyes, so like Kev's, met mine with an understanding look, and I felt better instantly. Lisa was sent off to get me a Diet Coke and I sat down opposite Bernie. She said, 'The kids have all been sick. It's their first time out.'

As if to bear out her words Fiona collapsed into a fit of coughing. It didn't seem to affect her appetite though, she took a massive bite of her doughnut as soon as she'd recovered.

Their mother sat beside me and sipped her coffee. She said, 'It's nice to see you again, Jackie.'

Feeling warmed by their welcome, I said to her, 'I'm sorry about your ankle.'

'It's fine now,' she answered. 'Bernie's been a great help, and Kev too.'

I felt a tremor just at the mention of his name.

Bernie said quickly, 'Kev'll be along later, he went to get paid for last night's gig.' At least he hadn't been with Sinead. Or maybe she'd been at the gig too. I pushed the thought away.

Their mum rose and rounded up the kids. 'We're just off to Crazy Prices. See you later.'

Bernie called, 'I'll catch up with you inside.' The two of us sat in silence for a moment.

Then Bernie said, 'I heard Sinead went for you on the bus the other day. She's such a cow.' I always got a shock hearing Bernie say that, she usually spoke so gently, like her mother.

She went on, 'Kev wants to know what she said. He's raging.' I could see she was really wound up.

I said quietly, 'Bernie, you're my friend and you've got to tell me the truth. Did Kev go out with her last Saturday?'

She looked straight at me. 'Look, what happened was, she went to Burgerama at eleven when Kev was finishing up. She got on the bus with him and talked him into getting off at the village and going into the club disco for a drink.'

'But he told me it'd be too late to go anywhere by the time he finished work.'

'Well, it was really,' answered Bernie. "Kev said she was shouting and giving out on the bus and he went along just to shut her up. Kev was wrecked. He only stayed a few minutes and then went off home.'

I considered this as we munched the kids' leftover bits of doughnut. It sounded possible. I could imagine the situation, and no-one knew better than I did how overpowering Sinead could be.

But if Kev cared about me surely he should make a complete break with Sinead? I was so fed up with the way she dominated all our lives. It was hard to believe that a few weeks ago I'd never heard of her.

Bernie said, 'I told him he should have given her the push there and then. But he hates scenes. He didn't want me to tell you, he said it was all over between them anyway.'

She leaned towards me earnestly across the table. 'Don't let her win, Jackie. He really likes you.'

I said, 'Bernie, Kev'll have to choose. I can't let Sinead go on messing me about like this.'

She picked up her bag. 'He knows that. He said to tell you he'd be outside Eason's around half eleven.'

I looked at her affectionately. 'What would I do without you, Bernie? I feel a lot better.'

She said, 'Listen, I'd better go and find Ma before those kids have her in bits.' She grinned, 'You tell Kev a few things.' And she walked off.

*　　*　　*

I headed upstairs to Eason's feeling great. I'd see Kev and I would feel the familiar feeling. I'd tell him how I felt about everything and he'd understand.

Soon I saw him coming up the escalator. He was wearing his blue sweatshirt and jeans. He was looking up, and unusually for him, he was smiling. I walked towards the escalator to meet him.

Suddenly there was a strong whiff of perfume and someone pushed past me violently. It was Sinead, of course, and as Kev got to the top she flung her arms round him and kissed him passionately on the lips.

I rushed off blindly. My eyes were full of tears. I knew this was it, I wasn't going to be humiliated anymore. If it ever had been love it was over.

The Exams

'Turn over your papers. You may begin.' Miss Kinsella sounded like the voice of doom.

I stared blankly at the English exam paper. I was relying on the Romantic poets, because almost the only things I could summon up from all the stuff I'd read and written about *Hamlet* were poor Ophelia drowning herself, and the ghost saying, 'Swear,' and they weren't going to get me very far. I hoped all the revision I'd done would come zooming back when I started writing.

But my mind was buzzing with everything that had happened in the past two days. When I got home from Ballytymon last Saturday I flew up to my room and took out all my books. I tried to put everything out of my mind except exams, but it was impossible. Questions kept raising themselves, and they weren't exam questions.

I'd remembered Bernie telling me ages ago that Sinead worked in a boutique in the Ballytymon shopping centre. But how could she have known where and when Kev and

I were meeting, or was it pure chance?

I kept seeing Kev's smile as he came up the escalator. Was it meant for me, as I'd assumed? Surely he couldn't have known that Sinead would appear? And what about that kiss?

I realised that Deirdre was right, the whole thing was hopeless if I couldn't trust him. But what about everything Bernie had said, surely I could trust her? Or was Bernie pushing Kev to go out with me, like Sinead said?

I looked round at all the bent heads. Deirdre was frowning and chewing her hair furiously. Ruth looked up and caught my eye, and we exchanged despairing looks.

With a massive effort I turned my mind to *Hamlet* and the Romantic poets and picked up my pen.

*　　*　　*

Everyone was subdued on the way home from school. We were all knackered.

The afternoon exam had been biology and to my disgust there hadn't been a single question on the earthworm. We kept telling each other how badly we'd done, though of course no-one ever admitted to having done okay.

To make matters worse it was a glorious evening without a cloud in the sky. It was even warm enough to sit out in the garden, but instead I had to huddle in my room revising *Peig* for the next day's Irish exam and trying not to think about Kev and Sinead.

At the bus stop Ruth said, for about the third time, 'I'm

sure I've got a temperature.' We all groaned, but not even Therese had the energy for a suitably sarcastic reply.

* * *

That evening I sat at my desk with *Peig* open in front of me. But no matter how hard I tried to concentrate, my mind kept spinning back to the events of Saturday.

Deirdre had phoned after I got home to hear about my meeting with Bernie and Kev. I'd never known her lost for words, but there was a shocked silence when, having made sure the kitchen door was shut and no-one could hear, I'd told her what had happened that morning at the Ballytymon shopping centre.

Finally she said, 'Well, at least you know where you stand now. Did you hear anything since?'

'Yeah, he phoned after I got home, but when Mum said a boy was on the phone I told her to say I wasn't available.'

Deirdre said admiringly, 'Wait till Therese hears that. What did your mum say?'

'Well, Kev phoned again a bit later, and she told me I ought to talk to him. She sounded quite sorry for him.'

'What did you say?'

'I told her I couldn't speak to him 'cos I was up to my eyes studying. She couldn't really object to that.'

Deirdre said, 'That reminds me, I'd better go and do some studying myself. My mum keeps telling me the exams start on Monday, as if I didn't know.'

I said, 'So does mine.'

After I'd hung up I went into the living-room, where Mum was helping Philip with his knitting. Well, Mum was actually doing the knitting and Philip was adding up his sponsorship money.

I knew Mum would have some questions for me. The phonecalls from Kev had put her on the alert. I glanced at Philip and gave Mum a warning look. The last thing I needed were comments from him. Mum followed me out, carefully closing the door behind her.

In the hall she said in a deafening whisper, 'What's going on, Jackie?' I wish I knew, I thought.

Aloud I said, 'Look, Mum, I'm really under pressure with the exams and everything. I'll tell you about it when things are all sorted out.'

And before she could reply I hurried upstairs and put on U2.

*   *   *

The next day, the Sunday before the exams, both grans came for lunch. Everyone was very considerate towards me. Well, everyone except Philip. He kept grumbling because I was excused from helping with the washing up.

Dad intervened. 'When you've got fifth year exams, Philip, we'll make sure you don't have to wash up either.'

Philip made a face. 'That's not for years.'

Gran said cheerily, 'Oh you'll be surprised how quickly time passes.' Philip gave her a filthy look.

The phone rang and Mum looked at me meaningfully

as she rose to answer it. I could see she didn't much want to head Kev off again.

But this time it was Bernie. 'Listen, Jackie, I can't talk for long, I'm in my auntie's house. Kev's in a desperate state, he said you wouldn't talk to him.'

I said quietly, 'Bernie, I'll have to finish it with Kev and me. I just can't compete with Sinead any more.' My voice was shaking.

'Oh please give him another chance, Jackie,' she begged. 'He's in work now, but afterwards he's going over to Sinead's house to have it out with her. She must have seen us in the shopping centre and followed you. Honestly, Jackie, it takes a lot to get him going but he's really wound up.'

I could feel myself beginning to weaken at the thought of Kev in a desperate state. Inside I could hear the table being cleared. They'd be coming into the hall at any minute.

'Bernie, I've got to go now, and anyway I'm up to my eyes with the exams. But I'm glad you rang.'

She said, 'I'll try and ring again. But remember, don't believe anything Sinead says, especially about me. She hates me, and she doesn't want you and me to be friends.'

I said, 'Bernie, we'll always be friends, whatever happens.' And I meant it. I'd hate not to see her again, or the kids, whatever happens between me and Kev.

* * *

So it was on top of all this that I found myself battling through the horrors of exam week.

And the other days weren't much better than the first.

I'd thought at least the exam pressure would stop me thinking about Kev, but it didn't. Everyone, especially Deirdre and Therese, even 'Dear Anne' for all I knew, now agreed I'd be mad not to finish it with him after all that had happened.

Maybe they were right, but I kept having dreams in which Kev and I were together again. Waking up to reality was depressing.

By Friday I was really stressed out. And that was the day that Dad chose to drop his bombshell.

The Bombshell

The warm evening sun poured in through the open window of my room as I messed around after tea on Friday. The exams were over, and I was listening to the latest Saw Doctors album which I'd borrowed from Deirdre. The shouts of kids playing football and the buzzing of lawnmowers floated up from the neighbours' gardens below.

The gang were going to Pizza Paradise later to celebrate the end of exams. I'd said I might go along, though I'd never felt the same about the place since The Scene.

Meanwhile, I was supposed to be sorting my schoolbooks and tidying my room which was even more of a tip than usual after the chaos of exam week. Then I planned to try out a new moisturising shampoo on my hair, recommended by Ruth because it wasn't tested on animals.

In fact, I'd only got as far as picking up my battered copy of *Français Aujourd'hui*. I was looking at the portraits

I'd drawn in the back, and wondering if Kev and Bernie and the Ballytymon crowd had gone out of my life forever.

In some ways I felt I'd only come alive properly since I'd met them. The future looked dull and grey now without them and all the ups and downs.

* * *

These reflections were interrupted by a light tap on my door. This was unusual. Mum certainly didn't knock whenever she came in, generally to leave me a pile of clean clothes and collect the dirty ones. And Philip's method of announcing his presence was to give the door a kick.

I opened the door. Dad was standing there.

'Dad, what's wrong?' I asked, astonished. He hardly ever came to our rooms.

He said in a low voice, 'Jackie, I just want to have a chat. Can I come in?'

'Of course,' I said, hastily clearing a chair. 'Sorry it's such a mess. I'm just going to start tidying.' But it was clear he wasn't interested in the state of the room. I sat on the bed and waited expectantly.

'I don't quite know how to tell you this,' he said hesitantly. He kept fiddling nervously with his tie.

There was a silence. I noticed that there was more grey in his hair than there used to be.

He said slowly, 'It's about my office. You know we're financial advisers, don't you?' I nodded, though to tell the truth, I've never been sure what financial advisers actually do.

He went on, sounding as though it was easier once he'd begun. 'You probably remember the other partners coming here for a drink last Christmas.'

I dimly remembered that one had been very tall and thin. He'd patted Philip on the head and Philip had made a face and had to be hustled out. All they'd talked about when I was there had been golf. I'd escaped as soon as I could.

Dad gazed out of the window. 'Well, you know that people often give their savings to advisers like us to invest for them. People trust us with their money –' He stopped.

For a dreadful moment I thought there were tears in his eyes. But he blinked and carried on. 'To cut a long story short, it turns out that one of my partners has been pocketing the funds which we were supposed to be investing for our clients.'

'You mean, he's been stealing their money?' I asked incredulously. It was like something out of the *Sunday World.* 'Can't you get it back?'

Dad gave a wry smile. 'That's the problem. He apparently gambled away most of it, and he's disappeared with the rest.'

'Disappeared?' I echoed. 'Surely the police could find him and make him give back what's left?'

'They think he's probably in South America,' said Dad wearily.

I asked, 'Is this anything to do with the discrepancies you were telling Mum about the other morning?'

'Yes, it was when the accountants came to check the books a few weeks ago that they discovered large sums of money were missing,' he explained. 'It leaves me and the other partners in a very serious financial position. Paying back that kind of money will take a lot of doing.'

He looked at me sadly. 'I'm afraid it's going to affect us in lots of ways, Jackie. We'll have to cut back.'

I thought, no racer for Philip, maybe no holidays abroad. Still we can live without those.

Dad continued, speaking fast, as though he was desperate to get it all out. 'When the financial matters are settled I'll probably be out of a job. It's not easy to find one when you're over forty. And then there's the mortgage. We might have to move to a smaller house.'

I stared at him, shocked. I hadn't realised it was quite that bad.

I thought back to the snippets of conversations about money, the arguments, the stray comments. I'd been so wrapped up in my problems with Kev that I hadn't given any of these more than a passing thought.

'How long have you known about this?' I asked.

'A few weeks,' he answered. 'I didn't want to worry you till I had to, though Mum knows of course. We decided to say nothing until your exams were over.'

I got up from the bed and gave him a hug. 'Really, Dad, you should've told me before. I wondered if it was just the business with Philip that had you so hassled.'

'Well, it didn't help.' He smiled and touched my cheek. 'I really hate having to burden you with all this. But I feel much better now I've told you.'

I said, 'We'll manage, Dad. I can get a holiday job, lots of my friends do, and we really don't need a big house for four of us.' I thought of Bernie and Kev and all of them, and the cheerful bustle in their small house.

Dad came and sat beside me on the bed. He put his arm awkwardly round my shoulders. We were both a bit embarrassed. Normally we didn't go in much for displays of affection except for a kiss on the cheek and the occasional hug. But these weren't normal times. I could see he felt relieved. He stretched out his legs. It occurred to me that this was the first proper conversation we'd had for ages.

'By the way,' he asked casually, 'whatever happened to that lad and his sister from Ballytymon? You haven't mentioned them recently.'

I was surprised he still remembered them in the middle of this new crisis. I gave him an edited version leaving out the parts about Sinead and Kev and me. I explained about their dad having left and their mother's problems and Bernie and Kev helping with the younger ones.

He listened carefully. 'They sound like good kids. And I can see it's not a bad idea to have a change sometimes from the friends you see in school every day.' His response was so different from the previous time. But, a lot of things had happened since then.

Dad stood up. He noticed my French book open at the drawings. I waited for some comment about defacing the book. But he just said, 'You've got quite a talent for drawing, Jackie.'

'When are you going to tell the others?' I asked.

'Poor Nana'll be the most difficult. She knows something's wrong, but not the full story.' He went on, 'She'll be upset for us of course. And she'll worry about what Sylvia and Maureen will think.'

'Maybe a visit to Marcel might make her feel a bit better,' I said wickedly.

Dad said, 'Now then, Jackie, no making fun of Nana,' but he was smiling, and he went downstairs looking more cheerful.

I leaned out of the open window, feeling the sun warm on my face, and reflecting that it was getting harder and harder to be positive these days.

The Fancy Dress Disco

When Deirdre phoned the next day to make plans for that night's fancy dress disco, I said nothing about Dad's news. I'd barely had time to digest it myself. There'd only been a chance for a brief conversation with Mum while Philip was watching TV.

She was staring into space when I came into the kitchen. I'd intended to take her mind off things by asking for suggestions about what to wear for the disco. But she was much too preoccupied.

She gave me a strained smile. 'So you've heard the bad news, Jackie. Dad said you'd taken it very well.'

I considered telling her I'd become an expert on all kinds of bad news recently. But instead I gave her a hug. Actually it was hard to know what to say. I tried to think of something positive.

'We'll manage okay, Mum,' I said. 'Maybe they'll find the partner and get back some of the money.'

She shook her head. 'Not very likely I'm afraid.' She

made an effort to sound cheerful. 'But you're right, we'll manage. I'll look for a part-time job. It would be a help, and it'd get me out of the house.' There was a silence as we both realised it might be a different house.

'As long as you don't let your highlights go, Mum, or you might be dragged to Marcel.'

She forced a smile. 'We haven't said anything to Philip yet. We won't be able to buy him a racer for his birthday.'

'He wants a Nintendo now, that's a bit cheaper,' I told her.

At that point Philip barged in. 'Sports Stadium' must have finished. Mum snapped back into action at the sight of him. 'Philip, it's time you did your homework.'

He pointed at me. 'Jackie could go to the fancy dress as Dracula, she wouldn't have to dress up at all.'

'Pig,' I shouted as he disappeared, laughing hysterically at his brilliant wit.

Things seemed to get back to normal fast with Philip around.

*   *   *

By the time Deirdre phoned I still didn't know what I was going to wear. She was fed up too.

'Everything's crazy here,' she said glumly. 'It's the Fine Gael dinner dance tonight and Mum's on the committee. People keep leaving things into our house.'

'What sort of things?'

'Well, they're supposed to be raffle and spot prizes but Dad says the neighbours are just donating their rubbish.

He's in Fianna Fáil you see. The doorbell never stops ringing and everyone's in an awful temper. I told them I was thinking of joining the Workers Party in protest, but Dad said it was only for people who work, so I wouldn't be let in. He thought that was hilarious.'

Then she said, trying to sound casual, 'Heard anything more from Kev?'

'Not since the time he rang and I never called back.'

Deirdre lowered her voice. 'Well, wait till you hear this. Therese dropped in after school yesterday. Bernie told her that Kev had a fierce row with that Sinead one.' She paused. Then she added, 'It looks like Kev thinks it's still on with you and him.'

On hearing this the usual niggling doubt came into my mind. Maybe I should talk to him one more time. And I really missed Bernie.

Deirdre continued, 'Therese said to tell you not to back down.' How did she know what I was thinking?

I changed the subject. 'What's Therese going as tonight?'

'Dunno. It's a big mystery.'

We speculated about this for a bit. Eventually Deirdre suggested we should all go round to Ruth's house, which was relatively peaceful, and sort out what we were going to wear.

'By the way,' she said before she rang off, 'They usually invite Mark's school to the disco, and Andy said he might come as well. It could be dodgy.' She sounded quite pleased.

I couldn't help thinking, Deirdre's going to have two fellas at the dance and I'm back to none. I felt the old stab of envy. I suppose it comes back when love has gone.

But if love was gone, why did I keep thinking about Kev? Was I always going to be haunted by my mystery man? Not even Dad's news yesterday could push him completely from my mind.

I didn't feel much like going to a disco.

* * *

At Ruth's house there were long arguments about what to wear. Ruth wanted us all to go as the Commitments, but we couldn't agree on what you could wear to look like them, apart from the usual disco gear that we'd be wearing anyway.

Ruth's mother came in to see if we'd like coffee, and she suggested we went as President Mary Robinson and her family. We smiled politely at this and made no comment, out of consideration for Ruth.

Then we sat around glumly for a while, listening to Bananarama. Ruth said we should be having herbal tea instead of coffee. Deirdre gave an exaggerated groan. I could see a row developing, but then Therese arrived and saved the day.

She'd brought a load of cheerleaders' gear that her cousins wore when they played in the Ballytymon Band. There were little short skirts, hats with pom-poms and tassels, and braid you could stick on.

'You could wear trainers and tan make-up on your legs,' Therese suggested helpfully.

We had some fun trying to twirl the batons and catch them. Deirdre was good but Ruth and I dropped them every time.

Tossing her baton down in disgust Ruth said, 'What about you, Therese, won't you need any of this stuff?'

Therese shook her head mysteriously. She turned her back on us and pulled on a bald wig over her short brown hair.

'Sinead O'Connor!' we all screamed. We were really impressed. Even Ruth's mother recognised who she was meant to be.

Walking home with Deirdre I reflected that friends could really take your mind off problems. I'd hardly thought about Kev the whole afternoon, or about Dad's bombshell.

I told Deirdre Dad's story on the way home. When she'd digested the news she said, 'Jackie, it's about time things stopped happening to you.'

'Yeah,' I said outside her gate, 'I can't complain about life being boring any more.'

*   *   *

Deirdre, Ruth and I arrived early at the school disco because Miss Kinsella had put us in charge of organising the raffle. The proceeds were to go to the Rape Crisis Centre, which was Deirdre and Therese's choice, and Greenpeace, which was Ruth's.

I'd have liked to include Concern or Childline, but I hadn't been assertive enough about it.

Deirdre's dad gave us a lift. It seemed to take forever to get there and Deirdre whispered that her dad was trying to escape from the preparations for the Fine Gael dance which had apparently now reached fever pitch at their house.

The familiar corridors of our school were dark and eerie as we hurried along to the gym. Ruth gave a little scream as a tall figure in a long green cloak with an Aran shawl over its head loomed in front of us. A voice said sharply, 'Did you remember to get the raffle tickets, girls?'

The shawl slipped down to reveal Miss Kinsella with her hair coiled into a bun. We were all dumbstruck.

'Don't look so shocked. Surely you know what character I am?' she snapped.

There was an embarrassed silence. 'Er – an old woman? I bet it's Peig,' Ruth ventured tactlessly.

Miss Kinsella glared at her. 'I presume you've heard of Kathleen ní Houlihan, the spirit of Ireland?'

'Of course, Miss Kinsella,' we chorused.

'It's very nice,' I added weakly as we carried on, restraining our giggles till she was out of earshot.

In the darkened gym another figure, with a tall top hat and a long black beard, was standing in the shadows holding what looked like a knotted rope. This time it was Deirdre who screamed.

I turned on the light. It revealed Mr McCabe, our

commerce teacher, blinking and holding a string of fairy lights.

'Turn off the bloody light,' he barked. 'You'll blow a fuse.' I switched it off hastily and we scurried out.

Breathless with laughter, we finally found a refuge upstairs in the kitchen. 'Have they all gone mad?' asked Deirdre. 'Who's he supposed to be?'

I noticed a table laden with dishes of crisps and nuts. We all started munching.

After a bit I said suddenly, 'Parnell.' They all looked at me. 'You know, they did it on TV, Parnell and Kitty O'Shea. That's who McCabe must be.'

Deirdre said, 'But wasn't Parnell good-looking?'

'He was on TV anyway,' I agreed. 'My mum was glued to it.'

'I wouldn't call McCabe good-looking,' Ruth said, confused.

'No-one said he was,' said Deirdre impatiently. 'Look, we'd better go and get busy with this raffle. Kathleen ní Houlihan Kinsella said we've to sell the tickets to people as they come in.'

Ruth said nervously, 'I don't fancy facing her again.'

None of us did. We sat on in the kitchen eating crisps, and fixing each others' tassels and pom-poms.

We were all having second thoughts about our cheerleader gear, though the red mini-skirts weren't bad. Anyway, we were stuck with them now. 'I'm not wearing that awful hat,' Deirdre moaned, 'and I'm not doing any twirling.' We all agreed on that.

After a while, voices and snatches of music floated up from below.

'Come on,' said Deirdre, 'Sounds like people are arriving. Maybe Therese's here. Or Andy,' she added casually.

'Or Mark,' said Ruth unkindly.

Or Kev, I thought, though I knew he wouldn't be, because of course it was all over between us.

I followed the others downstairs.

*   *   *

In the gym things were warming up. The coloured lights were flashing and Mr McCabe was fiddling with the amplifiers and counting slowly into the mike.

Avoiding him and Miss Kinsella, we went over to where a crowd from our class were standing about, a few of them with nervous-looking fellas in tow.

I was relieved to see that lots of people had dressed up. We'd been a bit uneasy about making a show of ourselves and then finding everyone else wearing their ordinary things.

Therese appeared beside me. Although we'd seen her in the Sinead O'Connor wig I still got a shock. Dressed all in black, with lots of eye make-up, the resemblance was startling.

She fished a folded note out of the waistband of her leggings and handed it to me. 'It's from Bernie. She made me promise to give it to you.'

I guessed Bernie had written to ask me to give Kev another chance. It was clear from Therese's disapproving tone that she thought the same.

There were too many people around for me to read it there and then and the cheerleaders' outfits didn't have pockets so I stuffed it in my shoe to look at later.

The music was blaring away now and a few people were dancing. Looking round I counted five Madonnas, two cats, and a devil which must have been left over from last year's Hallowe'en.

'No imagination,' said Deirdre scornfully, tossing back her hair. It was all very well for her, I thought, she looked great as a cheerleader, unlike Ruth and me.

The fellas showed even less imagination. There were a few wearing black hats who might or might not be The Edge, and at least seven in World Cup gear.

I asked Therese, 'D'you know if Andy's coming?'

'Some of the lads might drop up,' she answered vaguely.

Just then there was a stir at the door and a group of people came in, led by the hunky teacher I'd seen at the disco in Ballytymon where I'd first met Bernie and everything had begun.

I recognised the lad with the earring who'd chatted up Ruth. He'd let his shaved hair grow since the last time. There was no sign of Kev. I reminded myself I hadn't expected there would be.

I gave Ruth a nudge. 'Did you know the Ballytymon crowd were coming?' I asked.

She turned pink. 'Well, I was trying to distract McCabe one day from going on about my commerce homework being late, so I told him what their teacher said that time about us going to each others' school discos.'

As she spoke there was a ripple of laughter and applause, and we caught sight of Andy. He was dressed as Michael Jackson, complete with black hat, a black jewelled glove, and a metal-studded bomber jacket.

He swaggered in, bowing graciously, and then we saw the final touch. He was pulling a string attached to a small, rather battered monkey on wheels which must have belonged to someone's baby brother.

Even Therese had to admit he looked incredible. Everyone watched enviously as he came over to us. He held out his gloved hand to Deirdre. She clutched me and I could see she was practically fainting with excitement. I know the feeling, I thought wryly.

* * *

Things livened up after that. Ruth and I did the raffle, Deirdre was too busy with Andy.

'Just as well Mark didn't show up,' Ruth whispered as we crumpled up raffle tickets into a shoebox.

She was just starting to tell me she felt one of her headaches coming on when the lad with the earring came up to us. He was all in black. It wasn't clear if he was supposed to be anyone in particular.

He said, 'Howya, Ruth.' She turned to him with a big

smile, headache forgotten. I could see she was flattered that he'd remembered her name. I wondered if he was going to chat her up again with his charming story of puking on the Ramba Zamba. I told myself not to be bitchy.

It was difficult trying not to think about Kev, or about Dad's bombshell. But I was determined not to be a misery and spoil the whole thing for the others. I was going to enjoy the disco and worry about all the problems, financial and romantic, tomorrow.

And to my surprise, once I made the effort, I did quite enjoy it. We all danced together and there was a great buzz.

When we went to get a cold drink Therese jerked her head towards the dance floor. 'Did you see your woman?'

There was Miss Kinsella, her shawl slipping off her shoulders, her bun coming loose, jiving energetically to sixties music with the gorgeous teacher from Ballytymon.

We were still giggling when someone came up to me and said, 'Jackie, there's a lad outside wants you.'

My heart leapt in the old way. Could it be Kev, by some miracle? I hurried out, away from the heat and noise, to the entrance hall.

A small lonely figure stood there. It was Philip and he was crying. He flung himself on me, sobbing hysterically.

A chill went through me. 'What's happened?' I said sharply. Therese appeared beside me.

Philip gulped. 'It's Dad,' he stammered. 'He's had a heart attack. Mum said you've to come to the hospital straight away.'

'Where is he?' I asked mechanically.

'She wrote it down.' He held out a crumpled note.

For a moment I couldn't move. Therese took the note.

'He's in St James's,' she said shakily, 'In the intensive care.' We looked at each other. I'd never felt so terrified.

'I'll get one of the teachers to give you a lift,' she said, and rushed inside.

Philip was still crying. With a huge effort I said in a voice that sounded like somebody else's, 'It's okay, Philip, he'll be okay.'

Deirdre and Andy and Ruth appeared and they all stood round us protectively. Deirdre put her arm round me. No-one knew what to say.

I thought, please let this be a bad dream, and let me wake up and find it hasn't happened. But I knew it wasn't, and it had.

The Hospital

Much later that night I lay in bed and tried to make some sense of what had probably been the longest and most shattering day of my life.

The drive to the hospital in Mr McCabe's car had seemed to last for hours, though when I looked at my watch it was only about fifteen minutes.

I sat between Deirdre and Philip, who was sniffling quietly. Every few minutes Deirdre squeezed my hand sympathetically.

She had insisted on coming with me even though I'd protested we'd be okay. The others had wanted to come too, but Miss Kinsella said she thought it would be better for just one person to go.

In the car I whispered to Deirdre, 'I feel really bad about you missing out on the disco with Andy there and everything.'

She said, 'Some things are more important than fellas, even hunks like Andy.'

Mr McCabe kept saying encouragingly how much they could do for heart problems these days. I felt guilty about us calling him a male chauvinist. And I hoped he didn't remember how we'd nearly fused the lights. It all seemed so long ago.

He came into the hospital with us. The nurse at the reception looked at us a bit oddly. It was only afterwards that I realised how peculiar we must have appeared, a tearful boy, two bedraggled, white-faced cheerleaders and a man in a strange old-fashioned suit. Just as well Mr McCabe had removed the beard.

I gave Dad's name to the nurse and told her who we were. She spoke into a phone and directed us to the intensive care unit. The very sound of those words made my heart sink.

'How is he?' Mr McCabe asked her.

'He's holding his own,' she said briskly. At this Philip gave a sob and I felt a lump come into my throat.

As we walked to the lift I heard someone call my name. It was our family doctor, Dr Murphy, who'd looked after Philip and me through all our measles, mumps and chicken pox ever since I could remember. At the sight of the familiar tall figure with his thick glasses and reassuring smile, I almost burst into tears.

'Is Dad going to be okay?' I asked him, my voice shaking.

He said, 'They're doing everything they can, Jackie. Come on up, your family are all there, they'll be glad to see you.' He patted Philip on the shoulder.

I turned to Mr McCabe, 'We'll be okay now, this is our doctor. Thanks a million for the lift.'

'I'll get back then,' he said. 'D'you want a lift back, Deirdre?'

'No thanks,' she answered. 'I'll stay with Jackie.'

'You've a good friend there,' Mr McCabe said to me, nodding towards Deirdre. 'Keep your chin up. We'll all say a prayer for him.' And off he went, back into the world of normality from which we'd been wrenched so suddenly.

* * *

When we came out of the lift we were opposite swing doors bearing the grim sign, Intensive Care Unit.

Dr Murphy said, 'I'll just look in and see if your mother's with him.'

He re-appeared in a moment. 'You can go in and see him, Jackie. Philip and your friend can go into the waiting-room. Your gran is there.'

Dr Murphy must have noticed my fear, because he smiled at me reassuringly as we went in.

But it wasn't as bad as I'd expected. In the brightly-lit ward a young nurse was sitting at a table. She jumped up and brought us over to a curtained cubicle.

Inside Dad was propped up in a high bed. There were wires taped to his bare chest and hooked up to a machine with a screen beside him. His face was flushed and his lips a bluish colour, but incredibly, he was smiling.

Mum was sitting beside the bed holding his hand. I'd

never seen her do that before. She rose as we appeared and hugged me. She was trying hard to smile too, although I could see she'd been crying.

'Thank goodness you're here, Jackie,' she said. 'Dad's been looking forward to seeing you.'

As I bent over to kiss Dad he whispered, 'Sorry about ruining your disco, Jackie.'

At this, tears started to well up. 'Sorry,' I snuffled, trying to hold them back.

Dr Murphy said comfortingly, 'It's all right, Jackie, it's just the shock.'

Mum dabbed at her eyes and handed me a tissue. Then she looked round anxiously. 'Where's Philip?'

'He's with Gran in the waiting room,' I told her. 'Deirdre's there too.'

Mum said quietly, 'I phoned Gemma. She and Nana are coming up from Galway in the morning.' I'd forgotten Nana had gone to stay with my Auntie Gemma.

Mum must be really worried if she'd rung them in Galway, I thought. I could imagine the state Nana would be in. But Auntie Gemma was always cheerful, having her around would be a help.

The nurse said, 'I think our patient should rest now. You can come back later. I'll get someone to bring you a cup of tea in the waiting-room.' I noticed her hair under the starched white cap was thick, dark and curly, a bit like mine.

Dad gave a weak little wave as we went out.

In the waiting-room Gran sat with her arm round Philip, chatting to Deirdre. They looked up anxiously as we came in.

Dr Murphy addressed us. 'His condition is stable, but he's not out of the woods yet. By tomorrow morning all the test results should be available and we'll have a better idea of the prognosis.'

'That means, how soon he'll get better,' Gran explained to Philip in a whisper. She looked at Dr Murphy and said with a little smile, 'Positive thinking.'

But I was fairly sure 'prognosis' meant that he might not get better.

Another nurse came in with tea and biscuits. I suddenly felt hungry. Deirdre, Philip and I had the biscuits while Mum, Gran and Dr Murphy drank the tea.

A doctor in a white coat, who Mum said was the cardiologist, came in and said much the same as Dr Murphy, and suggested that we should all go home and get some rest.

He said to Mum, 'Don't worry, we'll phone you immediately if necessary. But hopefully, he'll have a quiet night.'

Mum said, 'We'll be back first thing in the morning.'

'As early as you like,' he replied. 'I'll meet you here at half ten, when we should have the results of most of the tests.'

* * *

It was nearly two in the morning by the time we got to bed. Getting undressed I found Bernie's note, which I'd put in my shoe at the disco. It was very short and just asked me to talk to her before I made a final break with Kev.

I was so tired that I couldn't think straight, especially about the Kev business. But I couldn't sleep. Thoughts rushed feverishly through my mind. I thought how brave Gran was, after all she was quite old, and Dad was her only son, yet she put such a good face on things. And Deirdre, and the others, even the teachers, how supportive they'd all been.

On the way home Philip had fallen asleep in the car. We'd dropped Deirdre home. I hoped Mr McCabe had remembered to phone Deirdre's house as he'd promised, to explain why she'd be late.

He obviously had, because her mum came rushing out to ask how Dad was. She was all dressed up in a snazzy black dress, and I remembered about the Fine Gael dance. That reminded me about the disco, and how Andy and the crowd from Ballytymon had come along and livened things up.

It was so weird the way everything was carrying on as though Dad's heart attack hadn't really happened. And yet nothing was the same. Even the bombshell about Dad's firm didn't seem to be so important, compared with the thought that he might not get better.

I wondered if the stress Dad had been through could have caused the heart attack. He must have been so worried. I remembered his comment about third level, and whether they'd be able to afford it now. I wished I could tell him it didn't matter.

As I lay there, my mind raced on. If it was a serious heart attack I knew Dad might die. I just couldn't imagine how life would be for us without him.

I thought of Kev and Bernie's mum, trying to cope as a single parent on Social Welfare.

How would we manage in that situation? Could I ever be as patient and calm as Bernie, especially with Philip?

These were things I'd never thought about before I met Kev and Bernie and the others. And now they were coming frighteningly close to home.

I forced myself to stop that train of thought. If Gran and Mum could be positive, so could I. After all, I'd learned from my visits to Ballytymon that you could have fun, and perhaps be a closer family even if you didn't have much money.

Before I finally fell asleep I thought how comforting it would be to talk to Bernie.

But the one I dreamt about was Kev.

The Crunch

I was woken up by the sound of a car drawing up in the driveway. Auntie Gemma and Nana had arrived. They must have left Galway at the crack of dawn.

I looked out. The sky was dark and heavy and it was lashing rain. It seemed appropriate.

The house appeared to be full of people and the phone kept ringing. Gran had stayed the night and was busy in the kitchen making breakfast for everyone.

There was no sign of Philip.

'He's still asleep, poor lamb,' said Gran, putting another batch of toast on the table.

It wasn't the way I'd normally describe Philip, but Gran always saw the best side of everyone. And I suppose it had been a big shock for him too.

I went to say hi to Auntie Gemma and ask how she was.

Then Mum appeared looking tired but calm. 'I've phoned the hospital,' she announced. 'He had a good night.'

Auntie Gemma said, 'I knew things would improve, Nana said prayers for him all the way from Galway.' She smiled at me.

Gran said, 'Never underestimate the power of prayer.'

'Quite right,' said Nana approvingly.

Just before we left for the hospital Therese phoned to ask how Dad was. 'Which hospital is he in?' she asked.

I told her, adding, 'If you're talking to Deirdre or Ruth could you ever tell them I'll ring them later when I get back?'

'Okay,' said Therese. 'By the way I hear Ruth's new fella's really mad about her, the one with the earring. She was going on at him about all the additives and stuff and how they're so bad for you and he told Andy after the disco that he was never going to eat junk again.'

I giggled. 'It must be great for Ruth to be taken seriously for a change instead of being slagged.'

I felt mildly comforted at the thought of Ruth and the others saying and doing the same things they always did.

*   *   *

As Auntie Gemma and I got into Mum's Starlet, it occurred to me that we might not be able to afford a second car now. I wondered if Mum could ride a bike. But I knew this wasn't the time to ask.

We'd persuaded Nana and Gran to stay at home and have a rest, promising to phone them from the hospital. We'd left Gran doing Philip's sponsored knitting while he had his breakfast. Auntie Gemma couldn't believe the knitting.

'You've got to be having me on,' she said when she'd stopped laughing. 'Has he done any of it himself?'

'Actually he spends most of his time adding up the sponsorship money he's been promised,' I told her. 'So far the total's come out different each time.'

One of the great things about having Auntie Gemma there was that she didn't make me feel we had to be serious all the time because of Dad. I knew she understood that just because I could laugh, that didn't mean I wasn't worried about him.

I stared out of the car window at the rain, thinking about the news we were going to be told at the hospital.

'At least this has put the office problem in proportion,' said Mum. 'All that matters now is that he should get better.'

Auntie Gemma obviously knew about the money troubles. She said, 'Heart attacks and hysterectomies certainly help you get your priorities right.'

We arrived at the hospital and Mum parked the car. As we got out Auntie Gemma linked arms with Mum and me. 'Come on now,' she said. 'Best foot forward.' And off we marched.

The young nurse met us at the door of the intensive care. Neither the name nor the place seemed so terrifying this time. She told us Dad had a comfortable night and had eaten a little breakfast.

'The cardiologist is with him now,' she said. 'He won't be long.'

We sat in the waiting-room and watched the rain dripping off the trees. We had run out of reassuring things to say to each other and a silence fell.

In the distance we heard voices and dishes clattering and the rattling of a trolley being wheeled down the corridor. There were a few out-of-date magazines on the table. Thinking of Deirdre I picked one up and looked for the agony column in case there was some useful advice, but it'd been torn out. Someone must have been desperate, I thought.

Then the nurse reappeared. She said to Mum, 'The doctor would like you to go in now.' Mum followed her into the intensive care.

Although Auntie Gemma and I tried to chat, we kept watching the swing doors. It seemed like forever. Eventually Mum and the doctor emerged, and stood talking for a few minutes.

I prayed, 'Please let him be all right.'

When Mum finally came back in she looked pale but she was smiling.

She took a deep breath. 'It's going to be all right. They say that although he had a cardiac arrest, there wasn't too much damage to the heart. They don't think he'll need a by-pass operation for the moment.'

Relief swept over me. I gave Mum a hug.

She went on, 'He's got to take it very easy, go on a

special diet, have regular exercise –' she paused. 'There was lots more. They'll give us a leaflet with information, and Dr Murphy's going to keep a careful eye on him.'

She paused. 'Oh yes, and they say it's very important for him to avoid stress.'

I had an overwhelming urge to laugh. 'Mum,' I said, 'how's he going to manage that in our house?'

Auntie Gemma said, 'Maybe when the holidays start you should all come to Galway for a bit.' She added, 'Mind you, even Galway's not entirely stress-free, not with my kids.'

The nurse appeared with yet another tray of tea. She heard us laughing and said cheerfully, 'Sounds like good news.'

As Auntie Gemma poured the tea, Mum said to me, 'Jackie, would you ever run down to reception and phone the grans and Philip to tell them the news. Then we can go in and see Dad.'

'Did they say when he can come home?' I asked.

'They're keeping him in for a while. But it shouldn't be too long.'

*   *   *

As I went down in the lift I felt more light-hearted than I had for ages. Maybe things were going to go right for a change.

Then I could go back to worrying about my lovelife.

I went over to the payphones beside the reception. As I inserted the coins I noticed someone with long fair hair standing at the desk. I knew instantly it was Bernie. Therese must have told her about Dad. I put the phone down and at the same moment she turned and saw me.

Then I looked past her and saw Kev.

The instant our eyes met in The Look as they had done at the bus stop long ago, my heart gave an enormous lurch and I felt dizzy. We walked towards each other in slow motion like the last scene in a film.

Kev flung his arms round me in a way he never had before, and I buried my face in his blue sweatshirt. I could feel his heart thumping. The warm glow surged through me, a feeling I'd nearly forgotten.

Then Bernie came up and we hugged each other and I told them the good news about Dad.

*　　*　　*

But whether it's really love, to tell the truth, I'm still wondering. Maybe you never really know for sure?